Back To Us

Teresa Roman

For my sister

Thank you for always having my back

Chapter 1

Nothing good ever happened to me without a little bad mixed in. Like the time I got hired to work at Radio City Music Hall over the Christmas season. I thought for sure I'd get to see at least a little bit of the Christmas show, but instead I got stuck outside working the doors and freezing my butt off.

My summer internship was apparently not going to be an exception to that rule. Between the ten-minute walk to the subway station and the three different trains I'd need to take to get to work, my mornings were not going to be fun. If it weren't for my absurd paranoia about being late I would've been freaking out as I waited for the A train that was apparently stuck somewhere in the tunnels under Manhattan. I still had over an hour before I needed to be at work, but there was no doubt in my mind that the ride from my crappy apartment in Brooklyn to my job on the Upper West Side was going to take a lot longer than I wanted it to. But still, it was a job. One that would look really good on my resume *and* help me pay my share of the rent. The extra money was coming at the perfect time, too, because frankly, I was getting tired of eating hotdogs and pecan sandies for dinner every night.

By the time I made it to the 87th Street Community Center, the back of my shirt was drenched with sweat and clung to my skin—thanks to another hot and muggy day. I took a deep breath and tried to ignore the nervous fluttering in my chest as I walked inside. The security guard looked bored and hot sitting behind a desk with only a small table fan to keep him cool. He looked up at me as I approached.

"I'm looking for Mrs. Connor," I said. "I'm supposed to meet her here at nine o'clock."

"Name?" the guard replied. He wore a navy blue uniform. The little gold nametag pinned to the left side of his chest read Donald.

"Jessica Maravic."

"Mara *what?*"

No one could ever pronounce my last name the right way. "Ma-ra-vich." I sounded it out slowly. Donald picked up the phone and pressed a few numbers.

"Girl named Jessica here to see you," he grumbled into the phone and then turned to look at me again. "She'll be right out; you can take a seat and wait for now."

"Thanks," I said before finding my way over to one of the chairs in the corner of the room. It had been about three weeks since I'd been to the community center for my interview, and I was so nervous then that I'd barely paid attention to my surroundings. There wasn't much to the entrance area. Just an old beat-up metal desk that Donald sat behind and a few scratched-up royal blue plastic chairs with chrome legs.

"So, you'll be working here?" Donald asked as he mopped his forehead with a handkerchief and adjusted his collar.

"Just for the summer."

"My name's Donald by the way. But you can call me Don."

"Nice to meet you." Something about the way he looked at me made me uncomfortable, but since I'd be seeing him almost every day for the next three months I managed to muster a friendly smile figuring I'd be better off if he didn't think I had an attitude.

"You live around here?"

I shook my head. "Nope, I live in Brooklyn."

Just then the door behind Donald opened and Mrs. Connor stepped out. She glanced down at her watch. "You're early."

"Sorry," I said as I stood from my chair. "I wasn't sure how long it would take to get here, and I wanted to make sure I wasn't late."

"That's fine. It gives me some time to show you around before the kids get here."

I followed Mrs. Connor down the hallway. She pointed to the restrooms and then poked her head through a door that had the word gymnasium stenciled on it. "Ah, you're here." I heard her say. "There's someone I want you to meet." She pushed the door open and walked inside with me right behind her. "This is Jessica," she said to the man standing in front of her. He was holding a basketball in his hands and tucked it under one of his arms to shake my hand.

"I'm Justin. Nice to meet you."

"I told Justin about you already. He usually helps me conduct most of my interviews, but he was out the day you came for yours. Justin's in charge of our sports programs here and pretty much the second in command. If I'm not around and you need something, he can help you."

"Nice to meet you, too," I said. Justin smiled and his amber eyes reminded me of twinkling Christmas lights. He had perfect teeth, straight and white like he'd worn braces when he was younger. He was handsome, there was no denying that. His hair was a deep brown, like mine, but what really stood out about him were the freckles that were scattered over the bridge of his nose and his cheeks like raindrops. I tried not to stare at him too closely, I didn't want him to think I was flirting, which I wouldn't do. Not on my first day at work, and not with a complete stranger, but in my experience guys were weird like that. You looked at them a second too long and they convinced themselves that they were your dream come true, and that was the last thing I needed.

"I guess I'll see you around," Justin said as Mrs. Connor and I walked off. She showed me the break room and her and Justin's offices next. Then we moved on to the computer lab and finally the classroom I'd be tutoring in for the rest of the summer. I was supposed to be helping high school students who'd gotten stuck taking summer classes with any subject they were having trouble with. I was also supposed to encourage the students to apply for college and teach them how to decide which school was the best fit for them. Mrs. Connor had a handful of summer field trips planned as well, and I'd be coming along with her on those. I'd gotten the job through the work study program at the university I went to and was really excited about it; not just because of the paycheck, but because I was an education major, which made it a perfect fit.

"Why don't you put your bag in here?" Mrs. Connor opened up one of the desk drawers and I deposited my belongings inside it. "Your first student should get here just after nine. She'll let you know which subjects she needs help with."

Mrs. Connor walked away, leaving me alone in the classroom. I was less nervous now that she was back in her office. It wasn't as if this was my first job. I'd had plenty of them, but I was always shy in new situations, and worried about making a good first impression. After I got to know people, I was perfectly fine.

I took out a notebook and some pencils and waited. It was almost ten before my first student showed up, and I couldn't help but wonder if she even wanted to be there at all.

"Come on in." I smiled and stood as she walked through the doorway towards me. I was trying to exude confidence and authority. A nervous teacher wasn't going to get very far. "I'm Jesse," I told her as she placed her backpack on the floor and took a seat.

"My name's Linnea." She reached into her bag for a book. It was covered with a paper shopping bag to protect it, so I couldn't tell what subject it was.

"So what do you need the most help with?"

"Everything," she grumbled.

I thought for a moment about what to say next. "Are you planning on going to college?"

"I guess."

"And what do you think you're interested in studying?"

"I don't know. Maybe nursing. My mom's friend is a nurse, and she makes a ton of money."

"You should pick what you like, not what you think you'll make a lot of money doing. Do you even like the medical field?"

Linnea shrugged. "I don't really like blood."

"You should probably try for a different major then," I said, trying my best to sound helpful and friendly, instead of judgmental.

"You go to college, don't you?" Linnea asked.

"Yes, I do."

"What do you want to be?"

"A teacher, eventually."

"Yeah, that ain't for me either." Linnea shook her head. "Can't deal with a bunch of wild kids. I do like computers though."

"That's good," I said, encouragingly. "But you need to be really good at math, what kind of grades are you getting?"

"Math?" Linnea slumped in her chair. "Not good ones."

"Well, then you're in the right place, because I happen to be really good at math."

Linnea finally cracked her first smile and a feeling of satisfaction came over me. Maybe I was getting off to a good start after all.

Chapter 2

Two more students showed up after Linnea. While I was finishing my third tutoring session of the morning Mrs. Connor poked her head into the room.

"Take a lunch break after you're done."

Without knowing if I'd have access to a refrigerator to keep my lunch cold, I hadn't brought anything with me, so I left the community center in search of something to eat. I found a pizza place a few blocks away; a slice and a soda wouldn't set me back that badly so I went for it because I was starving. It would be another two weeks before I got my first paycheck and I needed to be careful or I'd run out of money.

On my way back from lunch, Don, who wasn't at his desk earlier when I'd left for lunch, looked up from the magazine he was reading and grinned as I walked back into the community center.

"What's up, Brooklyn?" The flirtatious tone in his voice matched the look he had on his face.

"Hey Don," I replied curtly, hoping he'd hear the lack of interest in my voice and get a clue. I rushed in through the door behind his desk before he could say anything else.

I tutored three more students that afternoon. They all seemed wary of me at first, but after we started talking I could tell they began to feel more comfortable. It seemed crazy to me that not that long ago I was the one sitting in their seat. Now I was about to enter my junior year in college, and if you'd asked me four years earlier if I thought I'd be tutoring high school kids, I'd have called you crazy. The leap from someone suggesting that I should go to college, to applying, then getting accepted, and actually going was gigantic for me. Maybe that's why Mrs. Conner decided to hire me. During our interview I was honest with her and told her how hard things had been for me and that I wanted to make a difference in someone's life the way other people had made a difference in mine. As cheesy as it sounded, it was all true. And now, sitting in the community center talking to kids who were still so scared to admit they wanted more from life, I felt like I was doing it, making the difference I'd wanted to since I picked education as my major.

I left work that afternoon happy. My first day turned out better than I expected. It was so good in fact that I didn't mind the ride back home jammed into the train like a sardine in a can. When the train was that crowded it was unpleasantly hot despite the air conditioning, but the heat coming off so many bodies wasn't nearly as bad as some of the body odor that wafted through the air.

A much more pleasing scent greeted me when I opened the door to my apartment. My brother had left the remnants of his favorite Chinese takeout – spare ribs – in the Styrofoam container they came in. How he could eat that fluorescent pink meat I had no idea. There was also a half-eaten tray of General Tso's chicken, which was my personal favorite, but the baby roach crawling over it was enough for me to walk away from it despite the gnaw of hunger I felt.

I walked inside my bedroom and flopped down on my bed. My brother and I shared a two bedroom railroad apartment. It was small, consisting of my bedroom and his, a small entryway with nothing but an old futon couch for seating, a kitchen and bathroom. It was pretty rundown looking, the floors were linoleum and actually curled up in the corners of the rooms, but with New York rents being as expensive as they were, it was the best we could afford. I didn't invite people over very often because I was embarrassed by just how bad my apartment looked. The fact that my neighborhood was definitely on the sketchier side didn't help things either.

The door to my brother Mike's bedroom was closed, but I could tell he was home by the stench of marijuana wafting into my room from his. He seemed to think pot chilled him out, but in my opinion it made him paranoid and sometimes kinda mean, so I avoided him when I knew he was smoking. Besides, he was probably still pissed at me for adopting a cat from my friend Susan. Buddy needed a home, and I needed to get rid of the mice that were creeping me out. Roaches were bad enough, but mice were just plain nasty. I was getting tired of hearing my brother call me high maintenance every time one ran by and I screamed and climbed onto the nearest piece of furniture. Getting Buddy had been the best decision I'd made. I came home from class the day after he moved in and found three dead mice in the kitchen and I never saw another one in the apartment after that. To me,

Buddy was a hero and worth the price of my brother being pissed at me, but Mike was right to be annoyed. I should have asked if he'd be okay with it first.

I turned on my TV and flipped through a few channels, but didn't find anything of interest to watch so I got up and headed to the kitchen to make something to eat. A few minutes later my brother strolled into the kitchen, too.

"Hey, J. How was work?"

He actually remembered, I was impressed. "Good. I really like it. It's just a bitch getting there."

"Where are you working again?"

"Upper West Side."

"Oh yeah, that kinda sucks." My brother started clearing his mess from the kitchen table. "I left you some Chinese if you're hungry."

"Nah, I'm good. I had Chinese at lunch so I'm kind of in the mood for something else."

Telling my brother the truth, that I wasn't into eating food that had a roach crawling on it, wasn't worth the bother. He'd probably just give me his "so what" look, because if I was high maintenance, my brother was the polar opposite. Lying was easier.

"I'm heading out for drinks with Mel later, you wanna come?"

Melanie was my brother's girlfriend. They'd been dating for over a year, and Mel was really cool, like a best friend and a sister wrapped up in one. Normally I would have said yes, but I was low on cash and drinks were expensive. "I would, but I gotta get up early for work tomorrow, so I probably shouldn't stay out late."

"Never stopped me."

"Yeah, but you can get by on like three hours of sleep. I can't do that."

I finished eating the hotdog I'd made and gulped down an iced tea while my brother got ready to head out. About ten minutes later there was a knock on the door.

"See you later, J," my brother said as he went to answer the door.

"Tell Mel I said hi."

The house was quiet after Mike left, so I turned on the TV again, not really caring about finding something to watch, I just wanted to hear something other than my thoughts. Buddy must have sensed I was feeling lonely because a few minutes later he jumped into my lap. By midnight I was still up, sort of waiting for my brother, even though I knew he probably wouldn't be back for the rest of the night. No longer able to keep my eyes open, I fell asleep. In the morning I checked my phone to see if Mike had called. He hadn't. I loved my brother and I knew he loved me back, but he was pretty bad at showing it sometimes. It wasn't out of malice, I knew that, he was just kind of clueless sometimes. Things didn't occur to him. Things like "my little sister might be worried about me so maybe I should call her or text her and let her know I decided to crash at my girlfriend's house instead of coming home." Or maybe it was just me that was clueless, and I expected too much of my brother. But it was just the two of us, so sometimes I worried about him.

~

The morning air smelled like garbage, which wasn't that unusual on hot and humid days. It was like the air just sat still and the smells of the streets got trapped. By the time I made it to the train station sweat was dripping down my back and I was grateful that I didn't have to wait long for my train to show up because I was in desperate need of air conditioning. As luck would have it, I even managed to get a seat.

Just as I walked through the doors of the community center my phone started to chime. My brother had finally texted.

Sorry I forgot to text you last night, stayed at Mel's and probably will again tonight

The message made me feel better and I smiled.

"Message from your boyfriend?"

I looked up and realized Don was talking to me. "What?" I asked, even though I'd heard his question just fine.

"You look happy, just figured it was your boyfriend sending you a sweet message."

I couldn't think of anything to say in response. It wasn't really his business whether or not I had a boyfriend, and if he didn't work at the community center I probably would have told him that; but with me as desperate for a job as I was, I couldn't afford to piss him off and take the chance he'd say something to Mrs. Connor that would cost me my job.

"No, just my brother," I answered too quickly. It would have been better if I'd told him that, yes, it was my boyfriend, my very jealous boyfriend, texting me. At least that way he'd know I was off limits.

I rushed past Donald before he could ask any more prying questions. On my way to the classroom I bumped into Mrs. Conner. "I was just looking for you," she said.

"What's up?"

"The boys' basketball team practices this morning, and when they're done a few of the players will be going to the computer lab. I want you to head over there, get things set up, and when the boys show up, help anyone who needs it."

"Sure, of course, no problem."

It was another half hour before anyone showed up. I felt kind of bad sitting around knowing I was getting paid to pretty much do nothing. To pass the time I took out my phone and started reading one of my e-books. If I'd known I would have so much downtime I would've brought an actual book to read with me, I hated reading on the small phone screen, but it beat just sitting there doing nothing.

When I heard voices and laughter coming from outside the door I tucked my phone away and went to open the door.

Five boys, still sweating from basketball practice, walked in followed by Justin. "Make your way over to those computers over there," he said, pointing to the back of the room.

As the boys sat down in front of the computers, Justin turned to me. "Jessica, right?"

I nodded. "You can call me Jesse, though, that's what most people do."

"How's everything going so far?"

"Good," I replied, trying to think of something clever to add, but I was never good at making conversation.

Justin stood and looked around the room awkwardly for a few moments. For someone who coached basketball he wasn't that tall, only a few inches taller than me and I was right at average height. But he had strong broad shoulders. I noticed that even with the loose-fitting shirt he wore. "Okay, well. I…better get back to my office now," he finally said.

"We'll see you Thursday, right coach?" One of the boys called out as Justin turned to leave.

"No practice Thursday, remember?"

"Awww, man," a few of the boys replied in unison.

It turned out the boys didn't really need my help. They spent most of the time joking around with each other and talking about girls and acted like I wasn't even there.

"Mrs. Connor told me you guys were supposed to be looking for information on colleges," I said after a while.

"Don't need to," one of them said. "I'm going to whatever school I get a basketball scholarship at."

"Lucky you." I wished I'd done that. Maybe not basketball, but some other sport that gave out scholarships. Even with financial aid I was going to be over fifteen thousand dollars in debt by the time I graduated. But at least I'd have a degree, and that was a huge step up from the future my father had predicted for me.

"You're going to grow up and be a prostitute and die from AIDS," he used to tell me, even before I really knew what it meant. By the time I was old enough to truly understand, I wasn't living at home anymore. I'd been handed over to the state of New York because I was too wild and unruly, at least in my father's eyes. I wondered what he would have thought of the eight other girls who lived in the group home I was eventually placed in. At fourteen, I was still pretty innocent compared to my new housemates. That changed quickly and I wondered if I'd ever not be bitter about it. Although no matter how rough it was in the group home, it was still better than being abused by my father.

~

I ran into Justin again during my lunch break while trying to figure out how to get the dinosaur of a microwave they had in the break room to work. He was eating at the big round table in the middle of the room and must have noticed me having a hard time.

"That thing is a fossil," he said as he walked over to help me. "I should buy another one and bring it in, but I keep forgetting." Justin pointed to one of the buttons on the microwave. "You gotta press this one first before you do anything else."

"Thanks," I said feeling embarrassed at my inability to operate a simple appliance.

"No problem."

I turned to look at him. His dark hair was cut into a close-cropped fade, and I found myself wondering if he'd let it grow longer when summer was over.

"Did the boys behave themselves this morning?"

"Yeah. They were fine. But I kind of felt bad 'cause it didn't seem like they needed my help that much."

"Well, they might have been a little shy. Sometimes we boys don't like to admit we need help, especially to a pretty girl."

I didn't need to have a mirror in front of me to know that my face turned several shades of red. If those words had come from Don I would have been annoyed, instead I found myself feeling flattered, and shy.

"I'm pretty sure that wasn't it." The microwave dinged letting me know my lunch was ready. Justin grabbed it out of the microwave for me and brought it over to the table. I sat beside him not knowing what to make of his chivalry.

Before I could thank Justin, Don walked in, spotted the two of us and strolled over to give Justin a fist bump. "Hey Jesse," he said before pulling out a chair next to me.

"You two didn't want to be alone, did you? Am I interrupting something?" Without pausing for a reply, Don leaned towards me and said, "You know, Justin here, he's a real good man."

"Not as good as good as you, Don," Justin joked going along with Don's banter.

"And modest, too."

"Hey, c'mon, man. You're embarrassing her," Justin said. He apparently wasn't as oblivious as Don was to my discomfort at their conversation.

"Am I?"

"No, not at all," I replied, lying through my teeth. What I wanted to do was get up and finish lunch in my classroom, but walking away seemed awkward. I fell silent while Justin and Don started talking baseball. I didn't really have anything to add to their conversation. It wasn't that I didn't like sports, I just never had enough free time to follow who was in the playoffs or who was being traded to what team. Most New Yorkers I knew were die-hard Yankees fans, and summers were often filled with long conversations about the team.

When I finished eating I got up from the table. "I better get back to the classroom," I said, noticing that Justin and Don had stopped their conversation and were both looking at me. "I think I have a tutoring session in a few minutes."

I walked away and when Don thought I was out of earshot I heard him whisper to Justin. "*Damn*. That girl is fine."

I didn't get a chance to hear Justin's response.

Chapter 3

As I headed towards the train station that evening it dawned on me that the last place I felt like going was home. With my brother still at his girlfriend's there would be no one to talk to, unless you counted Buddy, but he couldn't exactly talk back. I sent a text to my friend Susan asking her what she was up to. Her boyfriend was over, but she wanted me to stop by anyway. Normally, I hated being the third wheel, but I was getting more and more used to it.

Susan lived in Bayridge, which meant an even longer train ride. When I finally got to her place she was outside walking a bunch of dogs. It was how she made enough money to quit her day job and go back to school; dog boarding and walking, which always struck me as funny since her boyfriend hated dogs.

"You look cute," she commented.

"Just got off work."

"Oh, that's right. At the community center? How do you like it so far?"

"It's good. I don't feel like I'm actually doing that much, though. I tutored a few people, but I've been sitting around more than anything."

"They're still paying you, though, right?"

"Of course. I wouldn't bother going all the way out there for free."

Susan smiled. She understood me. She hadn't had the easiest life either. Despite our almost ten year age difference, it felt like she got me.

I followed her back inside and climbed the three flights of stairs to her place. Her boyfriend, Greg, was sitting on the couch with a Sam Adams in his hand and the baseball game on.

"'Sup Jesse?"

"Not much, how's it going?"

"Good. The Yankees are up by one."

Baseball again. For a second my mind flashed back to Justin and Don talking earlier. I need to not think about Justin, I tried telling myself. He seemed like a guy who had his shit together, and those kinds of guys tended to avoid me like the plague. Instead, I seemed to be some sort of magnet for every dysfunctional loser in the five boroughs.

I flopped down on the couch next to Greg, he reached forward to grab me a beer.

"No thanks, I'm good." I hated the taste of beer and Susan was on her way back from the kitchen with a Smirnoff Ice, which she knew was my favorite.

"So have you met any cute guys at your job yet?" she asked as she handed me the ice cold bottle.

"NO! I'm not there to meet guys, I'm there to work."

"That's perfect," Greg chimed in, "'cause my friend and his girlfriend just broke up…"

"Whoa, whoa, whoa," I said holding my hands up to let him

know to stop talking. "First of all, I'm not looking for a boyfriend right now. I told you guys that, like a hundred times. And second of all, even if I was, I'm not going out with some guy who just got dumped."

Sometimes it felt like I was the only person I knew who wasn't dating someone. It also felt like everyone I knew was *always* trying to remedy that situation. But I just wasn't in the mood for dating. My last relationship had been a disaster of epic proportions. For months something in my gut told me my now ex-boyfriend had been cheating on me, but I didn't want to believe it. I'd given up my dorm room to move in with him and refused to admit how stupid I'd been to do it, so it took way longer than it should have for me to dump him. He was so used to me being a chump that he refused to accept my decision. He'd show up outside my classes and call me literally nonstop for hours on end every day, until I finally changed my number. It took months before he gave up, and thankfully, I hadn't seen him or heard from him in a while. I was *not* ready to go through anything like that again.

Greg was about to try and change my mind; I could see the words forming. Luckily, Susan stopped him. She shot Greg a look. "Leave it alone," she muttered before turning to ask me if I'd eaten yet.

"Not yet."

"You want to order a few pies?"

"Sounds good."

Even with the AC on it was hot. I held my bottle of Smirnoff Ice up to my neck and then my forehead to cool myself down and leaned back against the sofa cushions. It was another twenty minutes before the pizza arrived. By the time we were done eating, the game Greg had been watching was over.

"You want me to grab you another drink?" Greg asked as he stood and headed to the kitchen with a pizza box full of half-eaten crusts.

"She's already had two, and she's under age," Susan joked. "I don't want to be accused of contributing to the delinquency of a minor."

"It's too late for that." I actually would have drunk another bottle if I didn't have to work the next day.

Susan stood. "C'mon. I gotta take the dogs on one last walk for the night."

We headed down the street. Susan lived in an apartment over a sports bar that was pretty popular with a lot of the people that lived nearby. It was how she got to be friendly with so many people in her neighborhood. We stopped walking every few steps so she could chat with whoever it was that greeted her. Finally, after walking a few blocks away from her apartment the attention died down.

"You sure you're doing all right?" she asked.

"Yeah, why wouldn't I be?"

Susan shrugged. "You spend too much time alone."

"No I don't. I'm at work most of the day…"

"That's different, and you know it."

"Is this about me not having a boyfriend again?"

"No. I just worry about you, that's all."

"Stop, you're going to make me cry," I said trying to sound jokey even though I was actually being half serious. I wasn't used to having people worry about me, mostly because I never let anyone know they should. I kept everything that was going on in my life to myself figuring that no one cared. It was hard to throw off something that had become so ingrained into me. Ever since I could remember my father had told me over and over again, "The only people in the world who will ever care about you are your family because you're too pathetic for anyone else to give a damn about you." And that was before he decided he didn't feel like being my father anymore.

"That's the Smirnoff Ice. I should've made you stop at one," she teased.

I bumped her with my shoulder pretending to stumble around like I was drunk. And we both laughed. When we got back to her place I helped her secure the dogs and said bye to Greg before heading back downstairs and towards the train station.

~

The next three days at work were a lot like the first two. Except that there was no Mrs. Connor around, or Justin either. They'd gone to some leadership conference. Don's flirting got worse each day, and a few times I swore I caught him staring at my butt. He gave me the distinct impression that it wasn't going to be too much longer before he was going to make a move and ask me out. *That* was going to be awkward.

At least I was starting to get more comfortable around the students. One of them, a boy named Chris, came by for the second time that week. It was Friday after lunch. He was one of the boys on the basketball team. Around his friends he acted like he knew everything, but when it was the two of us, one on one, he opened up about how bad his grades were and how he knew, basketball scholarship or not, that he needed some help.

"How'd you get to be so good at math anyway" he asked.

"I don't know. I was always sort of good at it. I guess I just got lucky."

"Lucky and pretty, that's a good combination," he said. "Can I ask you something?"

"Sure."

"What are you?"

"What do you mean by that?" I asked, furrowing my brow.

"You kind of look Hispanic, but I'm guessing Greek or Italian."

I laughed. "None of the above." People guessed all sorts of things about my ethnicity, but hardly ever got it right. It seemed like most people thought if you were from Europe you had to be blond, unless you were either Italian or Greek. My brother actually did have dark blonde hair, but mine was chestnut-colored, like my eyes. Normally, I was pretty fair-skinned, but with all the walking in the sunny weather, I was already beginning to get a light tan. That sometimes threw people off when they tried to figure out where I was from.

"So where then?"

"I'm Croatian."

Chris leaned back in his chair like he was trying to get a better look at me. "Never heard of it."

"It's in Europe, near Hungary."

"My geography isn't that great either," Chris said trying to hide his embarrassment.

"Don't worry about it. Most people don't know where it is."

"You don't have an accent."

"That's 'cause I was actually born here," I explained. We were getting way off track, and I figured it probably wasn't a good idea to give out too much personal information about myself to the students I was tutoring. "Why don't we get back to math?"

After ending the day with my final tutoring session, I waited for Don to start locking up so I could duck out of the front doors without running into him. I wasn't going to be able to avoid him forever, though. I really had to figure out a way to get him off my back without making him hate me.

Chapter 4

Back at work the next week things got busier. Mrs. Connor wanted me to accompany her on a tour of John Jay College that she was giving to some of the students. I stood beside her in the classroom I used as she ran through a list of do's and don'ts with the students. Mrs. Connor's sing-songy West Indian accent held everyone's attention as she spoke.

"Any questions?" Mrs. Connor asked when she was done.

"I've got one." I turned my head towards the voice coming from the doorway. It belonged to Justin.

"And what would that be, Mr. Justin?"

"Mind if I come along?"

Mrs. Connor unfolded her arms that were crossed over her chest and let them fall to her side. "We're going to be doing a lot of walking."

"That's fine by me."

"Are you sure?" she asked slowly.

"Yes, I'm sure. You have a large group here, I know you could use another set of eyes."

"Well, you're right, I could. So, if you're sure."

I couldn't help but wonder why Mrs. Connor was making such a big deal about Justin really being sure he wanted to come along. It seemed weird.

"C'mon." Justin gestured with his hand. "Let's go."

We shuffled outside into the hot Manhattan air and headed towards the subway. Thankfully, rush hour was over and most of our group were able to find seats on the train, with the exception of me and a few other students. Instead, I grabbed ahold of one of the poles so I wouldn't fall when the train stopped. As the train started to take off I felt someone's hand touching my mine.

"Do you want my seat?" Justin offered.

"No thanks, I'm fine," I replied. A familiar flustered feeling came over me, sort of like the one I got when he complimented me in the break room the week before.

"So how was your first week?"

"Good…I think."

"The boys on the basketball team can't stop talking about their hot new tutor," Justin teased.

"Hey, I'm sorry," Justin said. "I didn't mean to embarrass you."

"No, you didn't," I replied, totally lying and feeling even more self-conscious that he'd noticed me blushing.

"So Mrs. Connor told me you're an education major."

"Yup, I am. Two more years and then I'm done. At least with my bachelor's degree." I glanced at Justin briefly. "What about you? Do you go to school or are you already done?"

"Neither." He shook his head. "I didn't go to college. I joined the Navy instead, but I had to get out because I got injured."

I smiled. "That explains the haircut." A mental picture of Justin in a Navy uniform came into my mind. I would've bet a million dollars he looked real good in it.

Justin rubbed the back of his head. "I guess I just got used to getting it cut this way."

"So how'd you wind up working at the community center?"

"After I got discharged from the military my parents kept pushing me to do something with my life, but I didn't want to go to college, and I couldn't find anyone who wanted to hire me so I started volunteering at the community center. After about a year Mrs. Connor hooked me up with a full-time job."

"Do you like it? Your job?"

"I love it. I love working with the kids and helping them find something else to do so they won't get themselves into trouble," he said. "I know it sounds cheesy, but the people I've met at the community center are like a second family to me."

"That's cool." I was still trying to think of something else to add when the train stopped at our station and we all needed to get off. I let myself drift towards the back of the pack of students and away from Justin. I was supposed to be convincing myself to *not* like him, but the more time I spent around him, the more I was finding it hard to ignore that he wasn't just cute, he was also really nice. Or maybe it was all an act. That's what guys did— made themselves seem perfect and waited until they lured you in before letting the ugly truth come out and I was damned if I was going to fall for that again.

We made it back to the community center just after noon, and by the time I went to retrieve my lunch from the break room I was starving. I stood in front of the refrigerator staring inside it for a few minutes, until I finally realized I'd forgotten my food at home. My wallet was practically empty since I hadn't gotten my first paycheck yet. There wasn't even enough for a slice of pizza, and I was both hungry and thirsty.

"Damn," I said slamming the refrigerator door shut. How could I have been that stupid? My lunch was sitting right on the kitchen table at home, but it wasn't doing me any good there.

"What did the refrigerator ever do to you?"

Could this day get any worse? Justin had walked into the break room just in time to catch my temper get the best of me.

"Nothing. Just pissed at myself because I forgot my lunch at home."

"It must have been a really good lunch." I didn't say anything. I knew he was trying to be funny, but I wasn't in a joking mood. "You know there's a million places to eat around here, right?"

"Yeah, right. I know that," I said leaning my back against the refrigerator and crossing my arms over my chest.

"Actually, there's a really good Mediterranean spot not that far from here. You wanna go?"

Mediterranean sounded good, actually anything sounded good. Justin must have sensed my hesitation. "C'mon, just say yes. It's my treat."

"Fine." I agreed only because I was hungry. I hated accepting charity even if the person offering it didn't know that's what they were doing. "But next time, it's on me."

Justin lips curled into a smile. "Deal."

I expected that we'd walk to wherever it was we were going, but outside Justin hailed a cab that took us about ten blocks away from the community center. If it was me, I would have walked.

Rent in NY was expensive, and I doubted that community-center pay left much behind after that was paid.

"This is the place." Justin pointed after we got out of the cab.

I followed him inside the crowded restaurant. We ordered our food at the front and waited at a table for everything to be brought out to us.

"I'm so hungry," Justin said after we got settled at our table.

"What did you order?"

"A few different things. There's some stuff I thought you might like to try."

I drummed my fingertips on the table and looked around. The place was busy and smelled heavenly, liked grilled meat.

"So, do you live around here?" I asked, conversationally.

"Not too far, I'm on the Upper East Side. What about you?"

"Brooklyn."

"Wow. That's a long ride in."

"It's not that bad," I said trying to sound cool and easy going. "I'd never be able to afford Manhattan rent anyway."

"If it wasn't for my parents I couldn't either."

"Your parents pay your rent?"

"No. Well—I guess in a way you could say that. I still live at home with them."

Our food arrived. The server put my gyro in front of me and then proceeded to fill the table with plate after plate. There was Greek salad and pita bread, hummus, falafel, shish kebabs. It looked like she'd just unloaded the whole menu on our table.

"A few things?" I said to Justin after the waitress walked away. "You ordered like the entire menu."

"Well, I wanted you to try my favorites. Whatever we don't

finish I'll bring back to work. Believe me, it will get eaten."

I picked up my gyro and bit into it. It was amazing. The warm spiced meat felt like it melted in my mouth.

"I'm waiting," Justin said, as I put my sandwich back down on my plate.

"Waiting for what?"

"For you to tease me about being twenty-five and still living at home with my parents."

"I didn't know you were twenty-five, but even if I did, I wouldn't make fun of you. It's sort of common in my culture to stay at home with your parents, sometimes up until you get married. At least most Croatians are like that. My family is kind of weird, though."

"What do you mean by weird?"

"It's a long story." And not one that I wanted to share at the moment.

One of the best things about going off to college was that I got to leave group home life behind and actually had a good reason to be on my own. When I was in the group home I got tired of being asked why a good girl like me wasn't living with her parents. It was a part of my life I didn't like talking about. Who wanted to admit that their own parents didn't love them enough? If your parents didn't even care about you, why would anyone else?

"So if you didn't think I was twenty-five, how old did you think I was?"

"I don't know," I said between sips of iced tea. "I never really thought about it."

"How old are you?"

"Nineteen."

"Nineteen?" He sounded surprised.

"I'll be twenty in another three months."

"Hmm, you seem older for some reason."

"Really? And why's that?"

"You just seem so responsible, so mature."

"You barely know me."

"I've seen you with the kids. You're only a few years older than them, but you're helping them plan their futures already. That's not something just any nineteen-year-old can do."

"Let's just say I've had a lot of diverse experiences in my life."

Justin looked up from his food. "I'd ask you more, but something tells me you're not going to answer me."

"And you would be right, so why don't we just talk about something else?"

"Yes. Perfect. Because there was actually something I wanted to discuss with you."

"You do?" I asked, worried that somehow I'd done something wrong at work. Technically he wasn't my boss, but he was my superior.

"I wanted to ask you about Don."

"What about him?" I tried to hide my annoyance at the thought of Don.

"I get the distinct impression that he's on the verge of asking you out."

"Why?" I asked, trying not to roll my eyes.

"Because he told me he was."

I put the piece of pita bread I had in my hand down. "I'm eating here." The expression on Justin's face told me he wasn't joking. "Oh God. He's old enough to be my dad." I was exaggerating a bit, but still.

"So I take it you're not interested?"

"Please don't tell me you thought I was, because I will be totally insulted."

"I was just checking." Justin smirked. "Some women like older men."

"Well, not this woman. Uchh. He gives me the creeps."

"If you want him to back off, I have the perfect solution."

"Really? And what would that be?"

"We could pretend the two of us are going out. He'll back off if he thinks I like you."

"He won't be mad at you for moving in on me?" I asked. "Don't you guys have some sort of man code?"

Justin laughed. "Nah, Don's a former Marine. I'm practically a hero to him."

"I thought all you military people had some sort of rivalry thing going on between the different branches."

"We do. But I was a Corpsman when I was in the Navy, and if there's one thing a Marine respects, it's a Corpsman. He'd still be calling me Doc if I didn't make him stop."

"What's a Corpsman, and why would Don call you Doc?"

"A Corpsman is kind of like what the Army calls their medics. We go out into the field with the Marines and if one of them gets injured we're there to give them first aid. That's where the nickname Doc comes from."

"I didn't know that." I felt kind of ignorant for not already knowing what Justin had just told me, but he didn't seem offended by my lack of knowledge. "Is that how you got injured?"

"Yeah." Justin answered. He cast his eyes downward. Clearly his injury was something he didn't feel comfortable talking about. I understood that, since I had a whole slew of things I didn't like to talk about either. The weird thing was Justin looked totally normal, no scars at all. If he hadn't told me about his medical discharge I wouldn't have guessed that he'd suffered some sort of injury. Although, when I really thought about it, earlier it had looked like Justin walked with a slight limp. Maybe he'd had some kind of back or leg injury. Or maybe I was just imagining the limp. Maybe what he had was PTSD. I didn't know too much about it, but I knew it was the type of injury that left people with invisible scars. An impulse came over me to reach for his hand across the table, but of course I didn't actually do it.

"So what does this pretend dating entail?" I asked, trying to lighten the mood.

"Nothing major. If Don sees the two of us spending time together he's gonna put two and two together, and just assume we're going out. And when he asks, I promise to be a perfect gentleman and not give him any juicy details about you."

"What juicy details?"

He shrugged. "The tattoo you have on your shoulder."

I laughed. "I don't have any tattoos."

"Yeah, but Don doesn't know that."

"True, and he never will," I said. "So I guess this means I owe you twice now."

"Twice?"

"Once for lunch and then for rescuing me from Don."

Justin smiled again. The way his eyes sparkled made it hard

to peel my eyes away from him. Good Lord, he was cute. Too cute, I reminded myself. Which meant getting involved with him wasn't going to be anything but trouble for me.

33

Chapter 5

Justin's plan to trick Don into thinking we were dating, thereby making me off limits, didn't take long to work. Don stared at me and Justin as we came back from lunch together, not quite holding hands, but familiar enough with each other that it got Don's attention. We ate lunch together in the break room for the next few days. On Friday, before I started my first tutoring session, Don stopped by my classroom. He walked inside and leaned against the doorframe with his arms crossed over his chest.

"So, you and Justin, huh?"

"Well, kinda." I wanted him to think we were together without coming right out and admitting it.

"You know, Justin's a real good guy. You be good to him."

"I will." Apparently, Justin had been right, Don really did seem to care for him genuinely. And for the past two weeks I'd been convinced that Don was nothing more than an old perv. Maybe there was actually more to him after all. Or maybe it was just the way Justin affected the people around him. Everyone at the community center knew him and seemed to love him. He chatted with the janitors the same way he did with Mrs. Connor.

He was friendly to everyone and when he asked them how things were going, it wasn't just small talk, he seemed genuinely interested. I envied his ease with people and, as the days passed, began to feel sort of disappointed that our little game with Don was just a game. I had to remind myself that even if I thought Justin was cute, it was better that he wasn't interested. My focus was supposed to be on finishing school, not the drama that came with dating.

The rest of June seemed to fly by. I'd fallen into a routine. Work during the week, and Saturday mornings at the laundromat. The rest of the weekend I got to hang out—mostly with Mike and Mel, sometimes with Susan and Greg, which did nothing to help me feel less like a third wheel, but it kept me busy. I'd given Justin my number in case he ever made it down to Brooklyn and wanted to hang out, but he never called. Our friendship was confined to the community center, and even though Don was still convinced the two of us had something going on, things between me and Justin were strictly platonic. The more time I spent around Justin the more I had to convince myself that it had to, it *needed* to, stay that way.

~

July Fourth wound up falling on a Thursday, which meant that the community center would be closed on both the fourth and the fifth, making it a short week at work for me. On that Monday I arrived to work early and bumped into Justin on my way in. Don wasn't even at the front desk yet, that's how early it was. Instead Justin and I ran into him in the break room pouring a few sugars into his coffee. Don and Justin exchanged morning greetings while I found a spot in the refrigerator for my lunch.

"So what are you two doing for the Fourth?" Don asked. He was looking at me so I figured he was waiting for me to answer, not Justin.

"Umm, I…I'm not really sure yet."

"Don't tell me you forgot the barbecue?" Justin said, sounding surprised and disappointed at the same time. He played his part well, sometimes I thought he enjoyed the little game we were playing more than I did.

"Yeah, right. The barbecue. I didn't forget."

Don glanced at his watch. "Oops, it's later than I thought, I better get up front."

"So what are your real plans for Independence Day?" I asked Justin when Don was out of earshot.

"You thought I was joking about the barbecue?"

"I figured it was all part of our "get Don to think we're dating" plan."

"Yeah, well, it kind of was, but now that I think about it, I'd like to formally invite you to my family's annual July Fourth rooftop deck bash."

"You guys have a rooftop deck?" I asked, trying to hide the awe in my voice. In my entire nineteen years I'd never known anyone who lived in a place with a rooftop deck. I knew they existed, but I didn't spend time with the types of people who had that kind of money.

"Well, my parents do," Justin said, then paused. "So what's it gonna be?"

I pictured what Justin's apartment looked like and my curiosity piqued. "I already told my brother and his girlfriend that I was going over to her family's house." And the truth was I didn't see myself fitting in with the rooftop deck crowd.

"So you're spending the day with your brother's girlfriend's family? What about your parents? They don't celebrate the Fourth?"

I laughed. My father's opinion of American patriotism wasn't particularly good. "Uhh, no. They don't celebrate July Fourth in Croatia."

"Wait a minute. Is that where your parents are now?"

"It's where they've been for the past five years," I replied, casually.

"Wait a minute." I could see Justin doing the math in his head. "You were fourteen when they left for Croatia? Who took care of you?"

"Long…"

"I already know what you're gonna say. Long story. Fine. I get it. But one day you're gonna tell me all your deepest and darkest secrets."

"Yeah, sure," I teased. "As long as you go first."

"So, if your parents aren't around does that mean you live alone?"

I shook my head. "No. My brother and I share a place."

"And what does he do?" I could hear the curiosity in Justin's voice and realized I'd said too much.

"He works for a company that does clinical trials during the day, and he takes night classes at Hunter." It was how my brother met Melanie, in a class they took together. "He's a Community Health major."

"That's cool," Justin said. He stared down at his shoes for a moment before looking at me again. "You're sure I can't convince you to come over? You see your brother all the time, anyway."

I laughed. "Truth is, I probably see more of you than him. But…I already told Mel I was going to her family's house, which means that she probably told her mother I'd be there. I'd feel bad not showing up."

"All right." Justin took a piece of paper from his pocket and jotted something down on it before handing it to me. "This is my address, in case you change your mind."

~

Wednesday morning started out a beautiful day, but by lunchtime heavy ominous clouds hung in the sky, and by the time I left work for the day it was pouring outside. I hadn't bothered to check the weather before I left for work in the morning which meant my umbrella was home where it was totally useless to me. A few raindrops didn't bother me, but the rain was coming down in sheets, so I decided to wait under the awning of the community center until it stopped.

Twenty minutes later the downpour had only gotten worse and I was half-tempted to just make a dash for the train station. The cool raindrops would probably feel good. Justin, who was just leaving work, noticed me waiting.

"Who would've thought it was going to rain like this today?"

Unlike me, he had an umbrella with him. "You must've."

"No." He winked at me. "I just keep a spare one in my office."

"And you're about to tell me this is my lucky day and you

have an extra umbrella for me," I said, half-joking.

"No extra umbrellas." Justin shook his head. "Why don't we just share a cab instead?"

"Sure, okay." The words came out of my mouth before I thought about what I was saying. A taxi all the way to Brooklyn would be expensive. I was getting regular paychecks, but a cab from Justin's neighborhood to Brooklyn was not in my budget. Before I could think of a way to back out Justin had already hailed a taxi. I reluctantly followed him inside.

"You all right?" he asked. I was terrible at hiding my feelings and, at that moment, I was mentally trying to calculate if I had enough cash on me to cover the ride into Brooklyn. Maybe I could ask the driver to drop me off a few blocks from Justin's and then I could take the train home from there. Pleased with the solution I'd come up with, I relaxed.

"I'm fine." I stared out of the window at the rain coming down. "Just hoping this rain clears up by tomorrow."

"There will be a lot of July Fourth plans that get messed up if it doesn't."

"Yeah," I agreed. The AC in the cab was either off or not working, and it was really hot and muggy, the worst combination. I reached into my bag for a hair tie and pulled my hair back into a messy ponytail. In the summer when it was really hot my long hair felt like a thick blanket on my neck and shoulders. As a kid, my hair was always short thanks to my dad's awful haircuts. In the group home I'd got my hair cut a total of one time in four years. It wasn't until after I left that I found out that the other girls and I were supposed to get money every three months for haircuts. Turns out one of the workers at the group home pocketed our money instead. Now I just didn't have enough extra money to spend on getting my hair done, so I just wore it long.

I looked at Justin out of the corner of my eye. He was wearing a t-shirt and his usual track pants. He always wore pants, even on the hottest days. I didn't know how he could stand it.

"Can I ask you something?" Justin's question interrupted my thoughts.

"Yeah, sure?"

"I know the two of us are pretending to be dating, but I was kind of wondering, do you have a real boyfriend?"

"No, no real boyfriend, just you, my fake one," I replied with a wry smile. "What about you? Do you have a girlfriend?"

"Nah. I'm not exactly what anyone would call prime dating material."

"What makes you say that?" His assessment of himself surprised me. We'd known each for about a month and I had yet to discover any flaws. Not only was he strikingly handsome, he was funny and kind.

"Uhh…guy who still lives with his parents." He held his hand up like he was introducing himself at a group meeting. "Remember?"

"Yeah, but you're cute enough to pull that off…I think."

"You think I'm cute?" He sounded genuinely surprised.

"Oh come on now," I said. "I can't be the first girl who's ever told you that."

Justin had no time to answer. The taxi pulled up to his building and he got out. Earlier in the week when Justin told me about his parent's rooftop deck I figured they had money, I just didn't realize how much. I didn't spend too much time in fancy

New York buildings, but I recognized one when I saw one. Justin finished paying the driver and waved to me as he walked inside his building.

"Your address?" the cab driver asked as he pulled away from the curb.

"Umm…can you just drop me off by the nearest train station?"

"Man told me take you to Brooklyn, he pay me for ride all the way to Brooklyn," the taxi driver said in a broken Indian accent.

"He paid my fare?"

"Yes, and big tip, too." For a moment I was too flabbergasted to say anything. "Your address, ma'am?"

"Oh yeah," I said before telling him how to get to my place.

On the drive home I dialed Justin's number. "You didn't have to do that."

"Do what," he asked, innocently.

"We were supposed to be sharing a cab," I said. "I didn't expect you to pay for my fare all the way home."

"Yeah, but it was my idea, it wouldn't be right to stick you with the fare."

"I guess I owe you again."

"Again?"

"Once for lunch, then for rescuing me from Don, and now this."

"You don't owe me a thing, Jesse."

"Yes, I do, and I always repay my debts." I wasn't exactly sure how I would with Justin, but I didn't like charity, and I didn't like feeling like I owed someone. If Justin was just about any other guy I knew I would've sworn he was just being nice because he wanted something, but Justin was generous with everyone. He regularly showed up with coffee and doughnuts for everyone at work. Sometimes he'd get pizza delivered to the community center at lunch and he never let anyone chip in. It was just his way, and it was starting to cast a spell over me despite my best efforts to talk myself out of it.

I was surprised to find my brother in the kitchen when I got inside our apartment. He sat at the table with a container of take-out in front of him. His hair and clothes were soaked and his fingers were coated with rib sauce.

"You should've just asked them to deliver," I said.

"Picked this up on my way back from the train station." Mike looked me up and down. "How'd you stay so dry?"

"I took a cab. Shared one with this guy I work with."

"You mean Justin?" I'd mentioned him to my brother a few times. I just hadn't realized he'd actually been paying attention to me at the time.

"Yeah, how'd you know?"

"I'm a guy, J. I know the way we think."

I frowned, not sure what my brother was getting at. "What's that supposed to mean?"

"The guy likes you. I can't believe you haven't figured that out already."

"You just say that 'cause you don't know him. He's nice to everyone, that's just how he is."

"Ok, whatever. But after he asks you out I expect you to tell me I was right."

My brother firmly believed that females and males couldn't be just friends. If a guy was being nice, it meant he wanted something, but hadn't worked up the courage to ask for it. I wasn't ready to admit that he was right, even though when it came to Justin I found myself sort of hoping he was.

"So what's Mel's mom going to do if it's still raining tomorrow?"

"You know Mel's family. They'll just bring the party inside."

Melanie came from a huge family. Her mom and dad weren't together anymore, but when they had been they'd made five children together who all still lived in Brooklyn. Parties at Mel's mom's house were always crowded affairs with loud music, usually a mix between hip-hop and merengue since they were Dominican, and lots of food. If it rained tomorrow someone would still be grilling, and the party would still be on one way or another.

Luckily, by morning the clouds and rain had cleared. Mel came over early and my brother helped her in the kitchen to clean and season some chicken that would get grilled later. By noon the three of us headed for the train station. I could smell grilled meat almost as soon as we got out of the train station. The music was already blaring by the time we got to Mel's mom's place. Mel and I brought the chicken she and my brother had seasoned earlier to the backyard before going back inside.

I found Mel's mom in the kitchen, half cooking, half dancing.

"Hi, Mrs. Vergara," I said.

She turned around and hugged me. "Go get some food, mija."

The dining room table was covered with a mixture of Dominican and American dishes. There was rice and beans, plantains and empanadas alongside hot dogs and potato salad. I helped myself to a plate of food and sat outside in the backyard watching Mel's brother and cousins playing dominoes. With all the beer at the party, it didn't take long for more than a few people to get kind of drunk. After yet another one of Mel's cousins suggested we'd make pretty babies together, I decided to go hunt for my brother.

I found Mel in the living room on the couch with her hands folded across her chest, she looked pissed. "Where's Mike?" I asked.

"Don't know, don't care."

That meant the two of them must have got into an argument. "What happened?"

"What happened is your brother is an asshole." Mel knew she could talk to me like that because half the time I agreed with her. My brother was a good guy, he never lied, and if you counted on him for something he always came through, but he could push a person's buttons sometimes. I understood him and I understood why, but that didn't always make dealing with it easier.

I sat beside her. "You okay?"

"Yeah. Just mad."

"And you don't want to tell me why?"

"Mike saw me talking to some guy and got jealous. We got into an argument about it so he went up to my brother's room with a few other guys to get high. He knows I don't care if he smokes, but at my mom's house…" She shook her head. "That's just not cool."

I couldn't argue with her. Truthfully, I didn't really care that much that my brother liked pot. He had a job and went to school, so it wasn't like it interfered in his life, but I couldn't stand the smell of it. And smoking at your girlfriend's mother's house, Mel was right, that wasn't cool. It seemed like Mike and Mel got into the same old argument at every family party. My brother had a jealous streak because, even though he never admitted as much, he was scared to death of losing Mel. She and her family had become his family, his anchor, and a part of him was afraid he wasn't good enough and that he didn't deserve her. A lifetime of hearing that from your parents tended to have that effect on a person.

I wasn't able to find my brother anywhere, and he didn't answer any of my texts so I said my goodbyes. I felt kind of bad leaving Mel when she was so upset, but she had her family—tons of cousins, her mom, her brothers, and Mike and I only had each other.

"If I see Mike do you want me to tell him to call you?"

"Nah, don't worry about it. He'll call." She sounded totally unworried, which wasn't surprising, Mel knew my brother was head over heels with her.

Going home to look for Mike was going to be a waste of time, I knew my brother well enough to know if he was pissed he wouldn't have gone home. He would have gone to one of his friend's to either drink or smoke some more. By three in the morning, I couldn't stay awake any longer. Mike hadn't shown up and he hadn't answered any of my calls or texts. The only thing I could do was pray that whatever my brother was up to he wasn't getting into the type of trouble he couldn't get out of.

Sometime before the sun came up my brother finally made it home. I heard him as he fumbled through my room in the dark on the way to his bedroom. I drifted back to sleep and woke up a few hours later. It took me a minute to recognize the noises coming from my brother's room. He was puking his guts out, probably from all the drinking he'd done. Mike ignored me when I knocked on his door—I went in anyway. He was lying in bed curled into the fetal position and he looked like shit.

"Exactly how much did you have to drink?"

"I don't know," he said, his speech slurred. "Four, maybe five, or ten."

He was making no sense. It was almost ten in the morning and he'd been home for a few hours already. Which meant that even if he'd been drunk when he got home most of the alcohol should have left his system already. That made me wonder if something else was going on.

"What else were you doing besides drinking?"

"Took some…" Mike pointed to his bedside table. "To help me sleep." He was speaking in broken sentences that I couldn't make much sense out of. There was a pill bottle lying on its side, completely empty. I picked it up and held it in front of my brother's face.

"What the hell was in here?" The label that had been there was torn off.

Mike didn't answer. I shook him to try and wake him up, but all he did was moan and try to knock my hands away. I stared at him for a moment trying to figure out what I should do. What if he'd overdosed on something? Panicked, I ran to my room for my cell phone. If I called whichever friends he'd been hanging out with they'd know what was in that bottle, but I wasn't sure who to call and my brother was too out of it to answer any of my questions. Before I was able to figure out what to do, my phone, which was still in my hand, started ringing. I picked it up without even bothering to see who it was.

"Hello." I could hear the panic in my voice.

"What's wrong?"

"Who is this?"

"It's Justin. Did I call too early?"

"No…no, it's not too early."

"You didn't stop by yesterday."

I glanced at my brother who was still and pale. I tried shaking him. "Mike, Mike." He didn't answer. "Can I call you back, Justin? Now really isn't a good time."

"What's going on? You sound really upset."

"It's my brother." I was too worried to keep my mouth shut. I felt like I was on the verge of tears, but I bit them back as I spoke. "I think he might have overdosed on something, but I don't know what."

"Did you call an ambulance?"

"No. I can't do that. What if they think he tried to kill himself or something and make him stay in the hospital?" I'd seen it happen more than once to some of the girls I lived with at the group home. "He'll kill me for doing that to him."

"Give me your address."

"What? Why?"

"I'm coming over. I can help you figure out what to do better if I see him."

"No. I don't think that's a good idea." I didn't want Justin seeing the neighborhood I lived in, much less the inside of my piece of shit apartment, and I seriously doubted there was anything he could do. Maybe he was right, I should just call the paramedics. "Besides you're not a doctor, you're a coach."

"I was a Corpsman in the military, remember? Believe me, I'll know what to do."

Mike turned on his side and let out a groan before doubling over and dry heaving. He probably had nothing left inside him anymore.

"Fine," I relented and gave Justin my address. Making sure my brother was okay was more important than Justin's opinion of me, and realistically how much longer could I keep up the façade I'd been trying to since the beginning of summer? It was only a matter of time before Justin found out that the two of us were not in the same financial bracket, not even close.

"I'll be there as soon as I can. Call me back if anything changes before I get there."

Every few minutes I got up and peeked through the window blinds to see if Justin had arrived. When he finally did, I ran to open the door to my building. He followed me inside and then into my brother's room. Mike was still sprawled across the bed, he seemed a little more awake.

"Oh shit, you weren't kidding. He looks like crap." Justin sat beside my brother and reached for his wrist. It took me a second before I realized he was counting Mike's pulse.

"Well?"

"His pulse is a little fast, but that's probably because he's dehydrated from throwing up." He turned towards my brother and shook his arm. "Hey bro, can you tell me what you took, what was in that bottle?"

"Zan…something." His eyes closed and he turned to his side. "Oh fuck. I can't remember."

"I can't make sense of anything he's saying," I said.

"It sounds like he's trying to say Xanax," Justin explained.

"What's that?"

"You really don't know?" Justin asked.

I shook my head.

"God, you're innocent. They're like sleeping pills." Justin reached into his pocket for his cell phone.

I grabbed his arm. "Who are you calling?"

"Poison control, they'll know what to do."

They came on the line a few seconds later and Justin started to explain the situation to the person on the other end of the phone. A minute later he was done with the call.

"Well? What did they say?"

"They said that Xanax is supposed to be short-acting. As long as he didn't mix the Xanax with a bunch of other stuff your brother should be better pretty soon. I can stay with you and help you keep an eye on him until he's more coherent."

"We don't even know how many of those things he took, though."

"The lady from poison control said it's pretty hard to overdose on Xanax. It's a sedative, that's why he's so out of it." I turned away from Justin so he wouldn't see the worried expression that was still on my face. He put his hand on my shoulder. "If he gets worse the only other choice is to call the paramedics."

"Oh my God." I sat on the edge of my brother's bed. "I can't believe he'd be this stupid." I covered my face with my hands. It wasn't even noon yet and I was already tired. Ninety percent of the time my brother was funny and nice and my hero. A year ago when I'd made the huge mistake of moving out of the dorms and in with my then boyfriend it was my brother who'd come through for me after our break-up. I had nowhere to go until my brother offered to give up his studio apartment in Alphabet City so we could find a two bedroom to rent together. There was no way I could've afforded a place on my own, and the dorm had a waiting list to get back in.

The other ten percent of the time my brother drank too much or smoked too much pot and wound up getting himself into trouble. He didn't see it that way. I knew that later on, after whatever pills he'd taken had worked their way out of his system that Mike would tell me I made a big deal out of nothing and that I needed to learn how to chill. One of us had to be the worrier though, because my brother seemed to think that no matter what happened things would work out, and I happened to know for a fact that wasn't true.

As a child Mike had been as damn close to perfect as a son could get, but after my dad decided he'd had enough of his disappointing children and pretty much abandoned us, my brother went wild doing all the things he'd always been too scared to when we were under my parent's roof. And when Mike got upset, which thankfully didn't happen too often, he got pretty self-destructive.

Justin sat beside me and placed his hand on the small of my back. "You all right?"

I sat up straight and took my hands from my face. "Yeah." I took a deep breath. "I'll be fine."

Justin's eyes darted around the room. He was probably wondering how in the world I managed to lure him to my ghetto neighborhood and rundown apartment. I waited to hear what was on his mind. "So you live here with your brother?"

"Don't be jealous," I replied, sarcastically, trying to ease the tension I felt inside.

"Well, I'm not going to lie. It's not the nicest apartment in the world, but…"

"But it's all I can afford for now. I have tuition to pay for and the job at the community center is great, but it's not exactly the best paying." I tried not to sound bitter.

"Your parents can't help you out at all?"

"They can. They just don't want to."

"I can't believe that. You're like a perfect daughter. You go to college, you have a job…and you're a really good person."

"How do you know I'm a good person?" Compliments made me uncomfortable, especially ones about my character. I wanted to be good, but most of the time I didn't see myself that way. I saw myself through my father's eyes. Lazy, selfish, shallow. It had been years since I'd seen my father and had to hear him say those things to me. Fourteen years of having him raise me had been enough to convince me it was true. For four years I was forced to sit through weekly mandatory counseling sessions at the group home, but the social worker assigned to me was more interested in staring at her manicure than helping me. "It's not like we've known each other that long."

"Long enough for me to figure that out about you. I see the way you are with the kids at the center. They really like you, you know."

"Really?" I turned to look at Justin's face. He seemed sincere as he nodded, but suddenly I was desperate to change the subject.

So…" I finally said after a few moments of silence passed. "How about we talk about you instead?"

"Sure. What do you want to know?"

"What was it like being in the Navy? Did you get to go to any fun places?"

"There was boot camp and corps school in Chicago. Then I got stuck at Camp Lejeune, or swamp Lejeune as everyone calls it, which sucked almost as bad as Afghanistan did."

"You went to Afghanistan? What was that like?" The truth was Justin was the first military person I'd ever met, and I found the whole idea of it sort of fascinating.

"Pretty boring." Justin's face went blank and after a moment he stood and started for the door.

"Where are you going?"

"To get your brother some water."

A minute later Justin was back with a glass of water in his hand. He was able to get Mike to take a few sips.

Justin sat back down beside me, the glass of water still in his hands. He wiped the beads of condensation off with his fingertips "So why won't your parents help you?"

"Long story."

"You always say that when you don't want to answer something."

"It's not like you've told me your whole life's story either. And we agreed that you'd go first, remember?"

Justin frowned. "I don't remember agreeing to that." Justin set the glass of water down on my brother's bedside table. "But since you insist, what else is it that you want to know about me anyway?"

"Well, I was kind of curious about your injury."

Justin looked at me, but didn't say anything.

"Is it PTSD? Is that what happened to you?"

He had that same faraway look in his eyes that he did when he first told me he'd left the Navy because of an injury. "Yeah."

There was a girl who stayed in the group home for a while whose dad had PTSD so bad that he physically abused her. When she told me the things he'd done to her I couldn't believe she still loved him, but she did. She'd visit him on weekends sometimes and came home crying when things didn't work out the way she wanted them to. My mother tried to convince me that's what was wrong with my dad too. Only she didn't use the words PTSD. She would just say that my father had been through a lot and that's what made him act the way he did.

I was about to ask Justin about his limp, but it was pretty obvious that he didn't want to talk about it so I didn't push. He picked up the glass of water again and gave my brother a few more sips to drink.

"Where's Mel?" my brother asked after he was done drinking. His speech was still slurred, but at least he was awake.

"I don't know. I haven't talked to her today."

"I need my phone," Mike said. He reached under his pillow and threw aside his blankets trying to find it.

"I really think you better wait to call her until you sound a little less drunk."

"I'm not drunk."

"Drunk, high, whatever. You'll just get Mel pissed off if you call her sounding like you do now."

Justin cleared his throat and I turned around. For a second

I'd almost forgotten he was in the room with me and Mike.

"I'm going to get us all something to eat while you two talk."

"You don't need to do that," I protested.

"Yes he does," Mike interrupted. "I'm starving. I'd like an everything-bagel with cream cheese, and an espresso, double shot."

I glared at my brother. "Ignore him, Justin."

Justin turned and headed for the door. "Got it," he said. "One-everything bagel. I'll just get you what I think you might like, Jesse, 'cause I know you're not going to tell me."

After Justin left my brother sat up in bed. He looked up at me with a smile on his face. "So that's Justin?"

"Yes."

"What's he doing here? I thought you two were just friends."

"We are. He called me while I was in panic mode about you and insisted on coming over here to help."

"Sounds suspiciously like a guy who's interested in my sister."

"No. He knows medical stuff, so he was just trying to be helpful."

Mike swung his legs around and reached for my hand. I resisted the urge to mother him and tell him to get back in bed, instead I helped to get him on his feet. "You know, you're impossibly naïve."

My brother was wrong, I knew a lot more about boys than he thought I did, but I didn't argue. In many ways he knew me best, but there was a chunk of my life that he knew nothing about, and that was probably for the best. Besides, it wasn't naiveté that kept me believing Justin wasn't interested. I couldn't bring myself to believe it was true, because what if it wasn't?

"Where are you going?" I asked as Mike headed for the door.

"To take a shower. I want to be dressed by the time your friend gets back with breakfast."

"Before you do that can you at least tell me what the hell you were thinking taking all those pills?" I said, my hands on my hips.

Mike sighed, then turned to face me. "I pretty much passed out after I got back home, but then I woke up too early and I was still in a shitty mood about me and Mel fighting so I couldn't fall back asleep. That's why I started taking those pills. My buddy Parker gave them to me a while back, he told me they were for sleeping. I took one, but it didn't feel like it was doing anything. So I took another one and then another. I probably should've just given them more time to work."

I shook my head and sighed. "Don't you ever do that to me again. You scared the shit out of me."

Chapter 6

By the time Justin got back, my brother was dressed and pretty much back to normal. Mike finished his bagel and coffee and went in his room, probably to call Mel.

"You don't need to stay," I said to Justin. "It looks like my brother has made a full recovery."

"You're sure you don't want me to hang out a little longer?"

"No." I shook my head. "It's okay."

There were no regular taxis that drove around my neighborhood, so I called a service to come and get Justin. They showed up about fifteen minutes later. I walked Justin outside. "Thanks for coming," I told him. "Looks like I owe you, *again.*"

"No. You don't." Justin brushed back some stray hairs that had fallen in my face. His touch was unexpected, and made me feel that crazy fluttery feeling in my chest that I knew meant bad news for me. "See you Monday?"

I nodded and Justin walked away. I waited until his cab was out of sight before going back inside. My brother was still in his room talking to his girlfriend. Suddenly I had an urge to get out of my apartment. I needed some air, having four walls around me felt suffocating. It was another hot day, but I didn't really care. My mind was too busy trying to process everything that had just happened, but the more I tried, the more frustrated I became. I walked towards the Fulton Street Mall figuring that the crowds and the stores would be a good distraction. It was about a twenty-minute walk from my house. I didn't have enough money for a shopping trip, but that didn't keep me from being able to browse.

By the time I returned home a few hours later my brother was gone. I didn't hear from him for the rest of the weekend, which I prayed meant that he and Melanie had made up.

On Monday, after arriving at work, Mrs. Connor came looking for me. She had a list of activities planned for the next two weeks that she wanted to talk to me about.

"We had a lot more sign-ups for the museum trips than I anticipated, so we'll have to go in two different groups. This week we go to the Met, and next week to the Museum of Modern Art."

It sort of surprised me that so many of the kids wanted to go on the trips, but I liked the idea of getting out, so it was fine with me. On Tuesday, me, Mrs. Connor, Justin and a handful of kids met in the gymnasium before making our way to the train station. I watched Justin as he walked in front of me. Even in eighty plus degree weather, Justin still had on pants. It seemed weird because he had the type of job where it was actually okay to wear shorts.

Justin turned around and I looked away before he could catch that I'd been staring at him. I weaved my way through the crowd until I was sure Justin couldn't see me. He called my name to get my attention, but I pretended I didn't hear him. We hadn't talked at all since he'd left my apartment on Friday and with my worry over Mike out of the way all I could think about was the way Justin had looked at my apartment. I felt too embarrassed to have a conversation with him. Not that it mattered—we worked together so it was sort of inevitable, but I could put it off, or at least I thought I could. It turned out I was wrong, halfway down the block Justin caught up with me.

"Hey," he said putting his hand on my arm. "Did I do something to piss you off?"

"What are you talking about?"

"You didn't hear me calling your name?"

"Over all this noise?" I said, covering. I didn't want him to think I was purposefully avoiding him.

Justin wiped his forehead with the back of his hand. "God, it sure is hot out here."

"If you knew we'd be going out in this heat, why didn't you just wear shorts?"

"I don't like wearing shorts. Can't get the ladies to stop staring at me when I do."

"If you do say so yourself." Without fail, Justin knew how to make me smile and laugh. He could turn anything into a joke.

Justin might have been joking, but I didn't doubt that what he said was true. Sometimes when Justin stood close to me and looked at me I felt like reaching out and brushing my fingertips across the freckles that dotted the bridge of his nose and cheeks. There was something magnetic about him, and it wasn't just the way he looked that made him that way. He had a soft, tender side that I found incredibly appealing.

On the train Justin and I sat beside each other. "So how's your brother doing?" he asked.

"Good. You saw him. Once that medication wore off he was totally fine." I felt a need to justify my brother's carelessness. "I know you might not really believe this, but most of the time my brother is a totally cool guy."

"Hey, I'm not judging. I've done plenty of stupid things in my life."

"Somehow I find that hard to believe."

"It's true," Justin insisted. I wasn't buying it, though. Although after he said it I realized there was a lot about Justin's life I didn't know and now that I had his attention it was a good time to ask more questions.

"Do you have any brothers or sisters?"

"Yup, two brothers, no sisters."

"You must be the baby." I wasn't sure why I thought he was.

"Actually, no. I'm the oldest. My brothers are a few years younger than me. They're both in college and…I'm the loser big brother who's still at home with his parents."

This time it didn't sound like he was joking. "I'm sure that's not how your parents see it."

The train screeched to a sudden stop slamming me into Justin. My body pressed against his. "Oh my god. I'm so sorry." My face felt flushed as I realized that I'd noticed how strong his chest felt and how good he smelled.

"Are you okay?"

"Yeah, I'm fine," I said, as I scooted back towards my seat. I wiped my forehead with my palm. "So do you get along with your brothers?" I asked.

"Yeah. We get along. I don't see them very often. Jeff, he's the middle one, has a girlfriend that he's always with, and James just started college last year so he's busy enjoying his new found freedom."

I wanted to keep talking to Justin, but we'd arrived at our destination and keeping a group of teenagers quiet in a museum was harder than I thought it would be. That explained why Mrs. Connor wanted to bring the kids in two smaller groups rather than all at once. I pictured myself the way I was just four years earlier, the age that most of the kids with us were. It was crazy how much I'd changed. Four years ago I was so angry at the world. Sometimes I still was, but nothing like I had been then. I couldn't imagine myself signing up to go on a trip like the one we were on, but if I'd gone, I probably would have been making jokes and acting stupid. Now I looked at the art hanging on the walls of the museum and found myself appreciating it.

~

It was either the field trips, or the knowledge that summer was more than half over that made the next two weeks pass by too quickly. I found myself willing time to slow down. Come the end of August my job would be over. I'd miss the kids and Mrs. Connor—and Justin. Maybe we'd keep in touch for the next few months, but eventually I predicted our friendship would fade. Brooklyn was too far from the Upper East Side, and with me back to a full schedule of classes and Justin still working full-time at the community center I doubted either of us would find the time to hang out. If he was interested in me, now was the time for him to act, but he didn't, and with each day that passed I was beginning to lose hope that he ever would.

On our last museum trip I noticed something wasn't quite right with Justin. He walked funny, his slight limp more pronounced than usual, and I would've sworn that I noticed an expression of pain pass across his face a few times while we were walking.

"Basketball injury?" I asked.

"What?"

"You look like you hurt your leg."

He shook his head. "No. I'm fine."

It wasn't just his limp that caught my attention. Justin was quieter, less conversational than he normally was. But it wasn't until he didn't show up for work the following week that I realized something was wrong. By Wednesday I finally broke down and called him, but he didn't pick up his phone. By Friday, when he still hadn't shown up for work or returned my calls I tried texting.

Everything all right?

I was surprised and relieved when he replied. *Yes*

Where have you been?

Vacationing in the Bahamas – don't tell Mrs. Connor though, she thinks I'm sick

Next time you're bringing me

Deal

I spent the weekend looking forward to seeing Justin on Monday, but he didn't show up. Whatever was wrong with him it had to be bad, he'd missed over a week of work, that wasn't like him. I was going through some serious Justin withdrawal. It was awful how badly I wanted to see and talk to him. I knew eventually he'd be back, but when? In the evening before I left for home I went to look for Mrs. Connor and found her in her office.

"I was wondering if you've heard from Justin."

"I have," she said, without looking up from her desk.

"He's been sick for over a week. Is he okay?"

"It's not my place to talk about Justin's medical problems." I took that as Mrs. Connor's polite way of telling me to mind my business and didn't bother her with any more questions. But Justin was on my mind as I rode the train back home.

I called him later in the evening, but he didn't answer. He stayed on my mind most of the evening and by the time I went to bed I'd formed a plan. On my way to work I'd stop at his place first with breakfast. I'd tell him it was repayment for all the favors he'd done for me. I had his address written down on a piece of paper somewhere, so I knew where he lived. With my plan to see Justin perfected, I fell asleep with the look I anticipated on Justin's face on my mind. He'd be surprised, but I felt fairly confident that he'd be happy, too.

I stopped for bagels and coffee on my way to Justin's feeling pretty good about my plan until I saw the doorman standing in the lobby of his building. If he announced my visit, it wouldn't be the surprise I wanted it to be. Luckily, sneaking past the doorman turned out to be no big deal, and I was able to get onto the elevator without him noticing. As the elevator zoomed to the top floor my heart pounded in my chest with the anticipation of seeing Justin, and his smile, and the way it made his eyes sparkle.

For weeks I'd been trying to talk myself out of whatever feelings for him I knew I had, but every day that got harder and harder to do. The past week at work had sucked without him there, and made me realize I wanted him in my life.

I rang Justin's doorbell and waited for him to answer, but no one came to the door. The piece of paper with his address on it that he'd given me just before the Fourth of July was crumpled in my pocket. I reached for it to make sure I was at the right apartment. I rang again and wiped my sweaty palms on my shorts as I waited for him to open the door. My heart sank as I realized that he probably wasn't home. Maybe he wasn't sick at all. Maybe there was another reason he hadn't been to work.

I rang the doorbell one last time and finally heard someone.

"Don't tell me you forgot your keys again." It was Justin's voice, I was sure of it. "You're always forgetting those damn things, you know how hard it is for me in this stupid thing."

The door swung open and on the other side of it sat Justin. In a wheelchair. Instead of the sexy legs he'd bragged about before were two stumps. He was an amputee, a double amputee. That explained a lot of things. Like why he always wore pants and why he'd been limping. It was the injury that ended his military career, not PTSD like he claimed. Or maybe it was that, too, because if I'd lost both my legs in combat I was sure I'd be pretty messed up in the head.

It was too late to erase the shocked look from my face. Justin had already seen it. Before I could think of the right words, actually any words to say, Justin slammed the door shut.

"Go away," he said from behind the closed door.

"Justin. C'mon, please just open the door."

"I said go away."

I wouldn't. I couldn't. I had to find a way to make things better, a way to let him know that his injury didn't matter to me. He didn't need to be embarrassed. I wasn't sure what to do. It dawned on me that if Justin locked the door I was pretty sure I would have heard a click. I reached for the knob, twisted it and opened the door. Justin sat in his wheelchair a few feet away with his hands covering his face.

"Justin. Why didn't you tell me?"

He dropped his hands from his face and looked at me with a mortified expression on his face. "Tell you what? That I have no legs. It's not exactly something I like to talk about."

"I…I thought we were friends." It sounded lame, but it was the only thing I could think of to say.

"Yeah, sure, friends," he muttered. "Maybe you think I didn't notice the look on your face after I opened the door, but I did."

"I was just surprised, that's all."

"And now you feel sorry for me, right?" he said, his voice mournful. "What are you even doing here?"

I held up the white paper bag and coffee. "I brought you breakfast. I thought you were sick, and I…I figured I'd surprise you, cheer you up."

Justin turned his head. "I'm not feeling very well right now, Jesse. Can you please just go?"

I didn't want to. What I wanted to do was put my hand on Justin's shoulder and tell him that legs or not I still thought he was one of the most handsome, sweetest guys I'd ever met. Instead I stood in the doorway willing myself to say or do something, but I was frozen.

"Jesse, please. I really want to be alone right now."

"I'm sorry," I mumbled it so quietly I wasn't sure Justin heard me, then I backed away from the door. Justin couldn't bring himself to look at me and eventually I turned and began to walk down the hallway. I heard his door close behind me and then I ran for the elevator and out of Justin's building without looking back. I threw the bagels and coffee in the trash before running towards the train station. I had to be at work in less than half an hour. How the hell was I going to get through the day? I thought about just going back home and calling Mrs. Connor to tell her I couldn't make it in, but I needed the money, and the distraction.

After arriving at the community center, I gave a wobbly wave to Don and went into the bathroom to wash my face. Did anyone else at work know about Justin? They had to. Why was it okay for Mrs. Connor and probably even Don to know about his legs, but not me?

Somehow I muddled my way through a morning and afternoon of tutoring. At the end of the day, as I was on my way out, I saw Mrs. Connor sitting in her office. I knocked on her door.

"Come in." I entered hesitantly. "Is everything all right?" she asked.

"Yeah. I just wanted to ask you something…about Justin."

She pointed to a chair in front of her desk and I took a seat. "What about him?"

I was afraid to ask her about his legs on the off chance that she didn't actually know, but that didn't seem possible. Justin said he'd volunteered at the community center for a year before he got hired. I doubted he could keep that kind of thing secret for so long.

"What happened to his legs?" I blurted the question out.

Mrs. Connor sighed and sat back in her chair. "I didn't realize he told you. It's not something he likes to share with most people."

"Is that the reason why he's missed work for over a week?"

"I told you already that it's not my place to talk about his medical problems."

"I know, but I promise the only reason I'm asking is because I want to help him."

"How do you even know he wants your help?" she asked, brusquely. It was a question I had no answer for. Maybe Mrs. Connor was right. "You know, I've noticed the two of you together. He seems to care about you a lot, Jessica, but you have to realize that some people have a hard time accepting help from others."

"So what am I supposed to do?"

"How did you find out anyway?" she asked. Mrs. Connor's face remained expressionless as I told her the whole story. When I was done she said, "My advice to you is to wait until Justin is ready to talk to you."

I didn't like Mrs. Connor's advice, but I decided to follow it anyway. Mostly because I wasn't really sure what else to do. The temptation to call or text Justin was overwhelming, but somehow I managed to ignore it.

Justin didn't show up for the rest of the week. By the weekend I was feeling bluer than I had in a very long time. Feelings of guilt and anger and a sense of rejection churned inside me creating an ugly stew of self-pity. Justin's silent treatment was unbearable. I wondered if he'd ever come back to work, and if he did would he ever talk to me again or would he do his best to avoid me? I hated not knowing where I stood with him, and I hated it even more that it was all my fault.

Even my brother, who most of the time seemed completely oblivious, noticed my bleak mood. "What's with you?" he asked.

"Nothing," I said as I stared at a plate of scrambled eggs I'd made, but couldn't eat.

"You look like shit."

"Have I ever told you how good you are for my ego?"

There was a knock at the door.

"Come in," my brother called out. Mel walked in and my brother handed her a coffee. She gave him a kiss and I couldn't help but grumble.

"What's with you?" she asked.

"Why does everyone keep asking me that?"

"What did you do?" Mel asked my brother.

He looked at her like he was clueless. "I did nothing."

"I'm just feeling sorry for myself," I confessed. Not like it wasn't obvious.

"Why? What happened?" Mel asked.

I told her the whole stupid story. How I'd been attracted to Justin since we first met, and how I'd gotten to know him and then thought he was really nice too, and even though I swore I wasn't interested in dating, I thought I'd show up at his place to surprise him and maybe, just maybe, he'd get a clue and see I was interested and ask me out.

"Oh, God. Don't tell me some girl answered the door."

I shook my head. "No. It's worse than that, way worse."

"What can be worse than the guy you like already being taken?"

"Oh, there are worse things."

"Like what?"

"Like finding out someone is a double amputee when they didn't want you to know."

"Whoa, whoa, whoa," Mel said, holding up her hands. "Back up a minute here."

"He was in the Navy. He told me he got injured, but he looked fine. I figured he just had PTSD."

"So this whole time you never knew about his legs?"

"He wears pants all the time. How was I supposed to know?"

"That's just crazy," Mel said, shaking her head.

"He was so mad at me. He could barely even look at me. I invaded his privacy, and he probably hates me now."

"He doesn't hate you," my brother said.

"And how would you know that?"

"'Cause I'm a guy, and I know the way guys think. He's embarrassed. Losing your legs is a big deal. He probably would've told you eventually, but now he can't, because you found out on your own. You've got to see things from his perspective. If he asks you out, and you say no he'll be crushed and think it's 'cause of his legs; but if he asks you out and you say yes, he'll think it's 'cause you feel sorry for him."

"Oh, great. Well, what am I supposed to do then?"

"That I can't help you with."

Melanie punched my brother in his shoulder. "Way to go, Mr. Sensitive."

"Hey, I'm just keeping it real."

I lowered my head onto the table and threw my arms over my head. "How is it that stuff like this always happens to me?"

"Good question, J." I felt my brother's hand on my shoulder, trying to comfort me. "I don't know when, and I don't how, but I have a feeling this thing is going to work itself out. I really do."

Chapter 7

Justin was finally back at work on Monday. As I passed by the gymnasium I heard his voice. I wasn't sure it was him at first, but then he spoke again and I knew. The first thing I felt was joy, but as the day wore on I became more and more upset as I realized he hadn't bothered to look for me and say hello like he always did. By the time lunch rolled around my blood was boiling. I felt like an idiot and knew the minute I saw Justin I was going to give him a piece of my mind, and the minute I started to do that I wouldn't be able to hold back my tears because that's what happened to me when I got real mad. I cried. And crying made me look weak and stupid, and I was angry at Justin all over again for making me feel that way.

I ate my lunch, or at least I tried to, in the break room. Justin was clearly trying to avoid me because he didn't step foot in the break room the entire time I was in there, and I almost always bumped into him during lunch. I decided to look for him and found him in his office. He didn't say anything as I stood in the doorway, he didn't even ask me to come in.

"Are you ever going to talk to me again?" My heart pounded

in my chest. Legs or no legs Justin made me feel things I didn't want to feel and the fact that he wanted nothing to do with me stung. My ego felt like it was tumbling down a flight of stairs collecting bruises and broken bones as it went.

"It was those field trips, all that walking," Justin finally said. His hand was tucked under his chin and he had a blank look on his face. "I went on them because I like talking to you, I like being around you, but all that walking…" He shook his head.

"What? What about it?"

"Everyone thinks it's not a big deal," he muttered. "You lose your legs then you just get a new pair and the next day you're running a marathon faster than you ever did before. But it's not like that. It takes a long time to learn how to walk on prosthetics, and it's not always comfortable." Justin sighed. "I got a skin infection on one of my legs, or at least what's left of it. I couldn't wear the prosthetic again until it healed and then they needed to make some adjustments to it."

"I'm so sorry. If I knew…"

"If you knew what? That my legs were blown off? You would have insisted I stay here like Mrs. Connor wanted me to instead of walking around the city like a normal person gets to do. And I hate not being normal. I hate that everyone feels sorry for me. I wanted you to see me as whole for as long as I could pull it off."

"Justin." He still hadn't invited me in to his office, but I took the seat in front of his desk anyway. "I still see you as whole."

He looked at me like I was the biggest liar in the world. "I shouldn't have been so mean that day. I'm sorry. I'd really like it if you could forgive me, and I'd like to still be friends."

There was that word. Friends. I figured after that day at his apartment that any possible chance I'd had with him was gone, but it hurt to hear him confirm it.

"Yeah." I choked back the lump in my throat. "Friends." I stood up and turned around stumbling on the chair that I'd just gotten up from. I braced myself and managed not to fall flat on my face and embarrass myself further.

Justin said something else to me, but I was too upset to hear the words. I rushed out of his office, down the hall and past Don as I ran outside to get some air. I leaned against the wall and closed my eyes. A few seconds later I felt someone's hand touching my arm. *Justin.* I opened my eyes hoping to see him, but instead it was Don. He must have noticed me running outside looking upset.

"Everything okay?"

"Yeah." My voice cracked. A dead giveaway that everything was not okay, but Don didn't ask me any more questions. My lunch break was almost over and I needed to pull myself together.

~

The next morning as I walked by Mrs. Connor's office she called my name. I stepped into her office to see what she wanted.

"Hey, Mrs. Connor."

She pointed to the chair in front of her desk. "Take a seat," she said, then got up to close the door to her office. I knew what she was going to tell me, ever since I'd found out about Justin's legs I'd been a mess at work, distracted and moody. Maybe someone had complained.

I waited for her to talk. "I know there's something going on with you and Justin," Mrs. Connor finally said.

"What do you mean?"

"He's not himself, you're not yourself, and Don told me that he saw you running out of here yesterday looking like you were about to cry."

"Don needs to mind his own business," I muttered and rolled my eyes.

"Normally I'd agree with you. And normally I wouldn't get myself involved in the personal affairs of my employees, but Justin is…he's special to me, and I can tell you're special to him, which, in a roundabout way, makes you special to me, too."

Gee thanks. "Things between me and Justin are sorta complicated, and I'm sorry if I've been distracted…"

"I'm not really worried about that. You've been great with the students this summer. They all really love you. You're on time, you've never missed a day. I have no problem with your performance."

"Then what's the problem?" I asked, confused.

"The problem is that I'm watching two people I care about hurting because they're putting obstacles in their path that don't need to be there."

"What do you mean by that?"

"I may be a lot older than you and Justin, but I can still recognize two young people who really like each other."

That was not what I expected Mrs. Connor to say. For a moment I was going to deny it, and insist that Justin and I were just friends. "He doesn't like me, at least not like the way you think he does. He told me himself he just wants to be friends."

"He's very self-conscious about his injury, Jesse."

"I don't know what I'm supposed to do."

"The way I see things there's only one option."

"What?"

"You're sure you really do like him and that you're not just feeling sorry for him?" she asked as if she were looking for confirmation that that wasn't the case.

"I'm sure."

"Then there's nothing left for you to do but fight for him."

Chapter 8

Fight for him.

Mrs. Connor's words rang through my mind the whole morning. I didn't know how to fight for other people. I'd spent so many years fighting for myself that I didn't think I had it in me to fight for anyone else. What if I lost? I didn't think I could stand it if I did.

After I ran through all the reasons why I couldn't put myself out there for Justin, my mind turned to all the reasons I could. He was worth it, I was sure of it. Maybe he didn't have the same feelings for me that I had for him, but somehow I had to find a way to reach him. A way to chase away the sadness I saw in his eyes and heard in his voice, the same sadness I lived with, even if it was for different reasons.

During my lunch break I found Justin in his office. I didn't wait for an invitation. Instead I walked right up to his desk.

"I thought of a way you could make things up to me for slamming the door in my face."

"Excuse me?" Justin sat up straight in his chair and looked at me with an expression of surprise on his face. That was good.

Maybe I'd get him to agree to what I wanted before he could think of an excuse to say no.

"You have to come to lunch with me. Pizza is my favorite, but I'll let you decide where you want to go."

"Jess." He'd given me a nickname—that had to be a good thing. "I don't think I'm up for much standing or walking yet."

"We'll take a cab, my treat. All we need to do is get you out to the curb. You can do that, right?"

"I don't know."

"Oh come on, Justin. Don't make me beg."

"Okay." He shifted in his chair and leaned forward resting his elbows on his desk. "On one condition."

I frowned. "What condition?"

"That you tell me why—why all of a sudden you're being so nice to me."

"What are you saying? That I wasn't nice to you before?"

"You've never invited me anywhere. I asked you to come to a barbecue at my house, you didn't want to. Every time we've done anything together it's been my idea."

"What do you want me to say, Justin?" I was starting to get frustrated and my pride didn't like the beating it was receiving from him.

"I want you to say you don't feel sorry for me."

I looked him straight in the eye. "I don't feel sorry for you."

Without another word Justin got up. I stood from my chair and the two of us walked together until we made it outside and into the taxi he hailed. A few minutes later the taxi pulled up in front of a pizzeria. We walked inside and ordered a pie to share. One medium pizza, just cheese.

"You sure you don't want any toppings?" Justin asked.

"Nope. I'm not a topping person. Except for jalapenos, but we're not at the right pizzeria for that."

"I thought I was the only one who liked my pizza plain."

Justin reached for his wallet. I pulled his hand away from his back pocket before he could get it out.

"Jess, it's not a big deal."

"Yes it is. You don't want me feeling sorry for you, well, I don't want you to feel sorry for me either."

I gave the cashier enough money for the drinks and pizza we'd ordered and Justin and I took a seat and waited.

"So since we decided we're friends again, I thought we should agree on something," I finally said.

"What would that be?"

"I think you need to start trusting me."

Justin looked like he was about to choke on his soda. "I can't believe you of all people just said that."

"Why?"

"Do you trust me?"

"Sure I do."

"Then why did you make me beg you for your address when you needed help with your brother?"

"You did not beg." Justin gave me a skeptical look. I sighed. "Fine, I admit it. I didn't want you to see my dump of an apartment. Especially after seeing where you lived."

"You really think where you live makes a difference to me?"

"If you lived in my apartment, would you be inviting people over?"

Our pizza arrived before Justin could answer. I reached for a slice and took a bite savoring the saltiness of the cheese.

"It's my turn to ask you a question," I asked as I put my half eaten slice down.

"Okay, shoot."

"Is the reason you're living with your parents because of your legs?"

That faraway look that Justin sometimes got returned. He looked away from me and I patiently waited for his answer. "Yes," he finally said.

"I'm sorry." It was lame, but it was the only thing I could of to say.

"It is what it is." Justin helped himself to a slice of pizza. The faraway look was gone, but so was his smile. I shouldn't have asked the question. What was I thinking?

"I'm sorry. I didn't mean to..."

"It's okay." Justin leaned forward. "There's something I'm wondering."

"What's that?"

"How ever did you get past the doorman and up to my apartment anyway?"

"It really wasn't that hard. You live in New York long enough without parents watching over you and you get smart pretty quickly. If I told the doorman I was going up to your place you wouldn't have been surprised, and that's what I wanted to do."

Justin laughed. "You definitely succeeded."

"I'm sorry I found about your legs before you were ready to tell me."

"Don't worry about it. It was hard hiding it, and I was going to tell you, eventually. You just caught me on a really off day and interrupted my one-man pity party.”

“You have every right to feel sorry for yourself.” I reached for Justin's hand and when he didn't pull it away I felt a small ray of hope start to form.

~

Things between me and Justin seemed to fall back into place. We talked and hung out like we had before, but something was different. Something intangible, but still very real. Justin smiled less, he seemed preoccupied. I was hoping he'd get a clue and figure out that I wanted him to ask me out, but he seemed further from doing that than he ever had been.

I was running out of time. It was only another few weeks that we'd be working together, and then it would be too late. Mike was sure that if I asked Justin out he'd say yes, but it wasn't something I'd ever done before, and I wasn't sure I had the guts to do it. But Justin was worth it, I finally decided, so I spent the weekend rehearsing what I was going to say to him. Nothing sounded right. Eventually I gave up trying to come up with the right words and decided that once I was in front of him the words would just come to me. By Monday, I'd made up my mind about what I was going to do. I left for work early and stood outside the community center waiting for Justin. Almost twenty minutes passed before he showed up and I walked right up to him as he exited the taxi that dropped him off.

“I need to talk to you.”

“About what?”

“I'll tell you later. Can you wait in your office for me tonight?”

He furrowed his brow. "What is this about?"

"You'll find out later," I said, and walked away before Justin could ask me any more questions.

The closer it got to the end of the day, the more nervous I became. I was tempted to pick up the phone and call Susan just to have someone I could talk to about what I was about to do. I hadn't told her or anyone else that I was going to ask Justin out. Just in case he said no I wanted to save myself from the further humiliation of having to talk about it after.

At five-thirty I heard the click clack of Mrs. Connor's heels as she walked down the hallway. As she walked by she saw me sitting at my desk.

"What are you still doing here?"

"I was waiting for everyone to leave so I could talk to Justin alone. Is he still in his office?"

"He usually says bye to me before he leaves, and he didn't today, so he's probably still in there."

I stood, smoothed out the front of my dress and inhaled deeply.

"You look really beautiful today," Mrs. Connor said before walking away.

The door to Justin's office was open. He saw me approaching and motioned for me to come in.

I walked up to his desk, my heart pounded in my chest and my legs felt weak so I lowered myself into the chair beside me.

"So, what do you want to talk to me about?"

"I…I just wanted to ask you something." *Keep it simple. And quick, to the point.*

"What do you want to ask me?"

"So you and I have hung out a few times, and…I always have fun when we do and I think you do too. So I was kind of wondering if we could do it again. I mean hang out again, but not as friends, I was kind of thinking you might want to go on a date with me, like a real date. I mean not boyfriend and girlfriend or anything, just a date and see how it goes." I was blabbering on more than I had planned to and Justin just sat there with a stunned look on his face. When I stopped talking he looked away. My heart sank.

"Why are you doing this?"

"Doing what?" The hammering in my chest made it hard to think.

Justin turned to face me. "You know I'm okay with us just being friends, I really am."

"Right, okay. That was…I don't know." I ran my hands through my hair. His rejection felt more crushing than I thought it would. I felt like crying, but I was already embarrassed enough. No, not embarrassed, humiliated. Without thinking, I got up from my chair and tried to make my escape with the last shred of dignity I had intact. Justin reached across his desk and grabbed my wrist.

"Where are you going?"

"Let go of my hand."

"Not till you tell me why you look so upset."

Another wave of humiliation washed over me. I grabbed my hand out of Justin's grasp. "What do you care?" I said, before bolting out of the door.

I was still angry when I got home. I slammed the door shut and stood with my back against it trying to process what just happened between me and Justin. I was too upset to eat dinner, but not too upset for alcohol. I opened the fridge, hoping to find some beers, but I was out of luck and slammed the refrigerator door closed just as my brother walked into the kitchen.

"What the fuck is wrong with you?" He sounded annoyed.

"Besides the fact that I'm a fucking idiot?"

My brother's expression softened. "What happened?"

"I took your advice and asked Justin out."

"He said no?" Mike asked, like he couldn't believe it.

"Not exactly." I sighed and folded my arms across my chest. "What he said was that he was fine with us just being friends."

"Oh shit, I'm sorry, J."

"So much for your theory about him liking me."

"Forget him. There's a hundred other guys out there that would kill to be asked out by you."

But none of them were Justin. "You know what? I have to get out of here." I grabbed my bag and ran outside. What I needed was to get enough drinks in me to forget what a total ass I'd made out of myself. If I asked Mike to get me something from the store he would have, but I just didn't like asking him for things.

Half an hour later I showed up on Susan's doorstep. One look at my face and she didn't even bother asking why I didn't call first. Instead she pulled me inside and I followed her up the stairs and into her apartment.

"What's wrong?"

"I'm such an idiot," I said as I threw myself down on her couch.

"Oh God, don't tell me you took that loser back."

It took me a second to register what she was talking about.

"What? No. Eww. I wouldn't touch him again with a ten-foot pole."

"Then what happened."

"I asked someone out, and he said no."

"Wait? What?" A shocked expression crossed Susan's face. "You asked someone out? How come I haven't heard anything about this guy?"

"I don't know. Maybe because I didn't want to start dating again, but I really like Justin, and I figured that after I stop working at the community center I probably won't see him that much anymore, so I felt like I needed to take a chance."

"And he said no? What is he? Blind?"

"He's not blind, and he didn't exactly say no, but he might as well have."

It was hard patching together a story for Susan without telling her about Justin's legs, but I couldn't tell her that part. Not because I thought she'd laugh or act weird, but it was Justin's secret, and I still felt kind of bad for telling my brother and Melanie about it.

"Jesse, you're really pretty. Maybe he just couldn't believe that you could be interested in him."

"I'm not that pretty."

"Yes, you are. You have *the* perfect body and perfect hair, and that whole exotic "I'm not from America" look going on that guys love."

"Well, maybe he's into all-American girls," I said, pouting.

Susan got up and went into her kitchen. A minute later she was back with two glasses in her hands, she handed me one.

"Coke?" I asked. I'd been hoping for another Smirnoff Ice.

"With rum, plenty of it, too."

I took a sip, then a gulp. It was perfect, and exactly what I needed.

"So what are you going to do?" Susan asked.

"Nothing. There's nothing to do. Justin probably thinks I'm not good enough for him, and he's right. You should see the building he lives in."

"If he was like that, then why would he be working at the community center?"

"Working with a bunch of poor kids at a community center is not the same thing as dating some girl who lives in a cockroach-infested apartment and can barely afford her rent," I argued, even though I knew Susan had a point.

One of the reasons I liked Justin so much was because of the way he was with the kids at the community center. He probably didn't really need to work at all, but for some reason he did, and he seemed to love his job. He knew *all* the kid's names and they all really liked him. So if the whole social status thing wasn't a big deal to him, then he'd turned me down for another reason. Maybe he just wasn't interested. Maybe he liked blondes or skinnier girls. I wasn't what anyone would call fat, but I definitely filled out a pair of jeans.

After three rum and cokes Susan cut me off, although I could've sworn the last one was mostly coke with just a splash of rum. I was tipsy, but definitely not drunk, and I wanted to be. It sucked being nineteen and not being able to buy your own alcohol.

Susan wanted me to crash on her couch, but I decided to go home instead on the off chance that my brother stocked up on beers while I was gone. He wasn't home, the refrigerator was as empty as I'd left it and it was way too quiet in the apartment. I turned the TV on just for some noise and fell asleep eventually, still in my clothes. The next thing I knew my alarm was going off. It pounded in rhythm with the stabbing headache I woke up with. I willed myself to get out of bed, but I just couldn't. Not just because of my headache either, I couldn't face Justin, not with a hangover, and not after what had happened the day before.

I called work and left a message saying I was sick. Mrs. Connor would put two and two together, but I didn't really care. With the covers pulled back over my head I sank back into a dreamless sleep and woke up a few hours later to the sound of my phone buzzing.

Five missed calls. Three from Justin, one from Mrs. Connor and one from Susan. Justin had also left two text messages.

Are you okay?

And

I'm assuming you're not answering your phone because you're not feeling well and need to rest, but if I don't hear from you by the end of the day I'm coming over.

The last text made me unleash a barrage of profane words. Angry as I was I texted back because I didn't want Justin to make good on his promise to come over. The last thing I was in the mood for was facing him.

I'm fine. Just have a stomach bug. Nothing to worry about.

Three more weeks. That's how long I had left at the community center. I could handle the humiliation. With some careful planning, I could probably manage to avoid Justin altogether. I'd get to work early, before he usually arrived and stay away from the break room. Three weeks of nothing but pizza and hotdogs for lunch was totally manageable.

I stayed in bed most of the rest of the day and only got up when my brother came home from work.

"I got you General Tso's," Mike announced as he came inside, "and your favorite Ben and Jerry's flavor."

I could have hugged him. Instead, I dove right into dinner and dessert.

"You didn't go to work today?"

I shook my head as I filled my mouth with a spoon of ice cream. "Nope."

"Don't let him do that to you, J. He's not worth it."

"It's okay," I said, feeling good for the first time since Justin's rejection. Maybe it was the ice cream or lying around in bed all day that did it. "I'm over it."

Or so I thought.

Chapter 9

Wednesday and Thursday passed and my plan to avoid Justin went off without a hitch. I only saw him fleetingly in the hallway at work as I ran outside for lunch, too fast for him to try and strike up a conversation. I tried not to think too much about the fact that he hadn't come to look for me in my classroom. My ego was already bruised enough without dwelling on that fact. Instead, I occupied my mind with thoughts of the upcoming fall semester. I'd registered for a full load of classes, and when they started I'd be too busy to think about Justin.

Friday came. Just like I'd done the two days before I'd arrived at work early to avoid running into Justin. But when I walked into my classroom there he was, as gorgeous, more actually, than I remembered, even though it had only been a few days since we'd last spoken. My heart thumped in my chest and I swore under my breath. I was only here for two more weeks, why couldn't he just have stayed away?

Justin stared at me. I stood still for a moment, not sure what to do, then I averted my eyes from his and walked over to my desk. I stashed my purse into the same drawer that I always did and pretended like he wasn't in the room at all.

"Do you mind telling me what's going on with you?"

"I don't know what you're talking about," I said as I took a seat behind my desk.

"You're avoiding me."

"Yes, well I guess I don't take rejection that easily. It's not exactly something that I'm used to. Sorry if that bothers you."

"I didn't reject you." Justin put his hands down on the edge of my desk and leaned forward shortening the distance between us.

"I have a student coming in a few minutes. This isn't the right time."

"Your student can wait, I'm sure she won't mind."

"Well, I mind. I'm here to work, not socialize."

"Jess…"

There was a knock on the door. One of my students, Olivia, had shown up.

"I know I'm early. I can come back later if you want me to."

"Yes, Olivia," Justin said. "That would be great."

"No, it would not." I looked up at Justin. "Justin, please. I don't want to do this again."

Something simmered in Justin's eyes, I wasn't quite sure what, maybe anger. He walked away without another word to me.

"Bye, coach," Olivia said, as he glided past her.

"See you later, Olive."

"You know he's the only one allowed to call me that." Olivia took a seat and started emptying her books onto the table. "He's cute for a white boy. I think half the girls on the team have a crush on him."

I couldn't help but laugh. But at the same time I felt sad. That was Justin. He drew people to him, all types. I loved that about him. All of a sudden, I began to feel bad for the way I'd acted for the past two days. I was being a brat just because Justin didn't want to date me. We'd been friends before, and just because he didn't see me the way I saw him, I shut him out. What kind of friend did that? I vowed that at the end of the day I'd find Justin and tell him I was sorry, and that I was also okay with us just being friends.

"You know I'm pretty sure Coach Justin likes you." I barely registered what Olivia said, I was so lost in my thoughts.

"What? Why do you say that?"

"He stares at you when you're not looking, and he's always asking about you, and telling us to make sure we treat you nice."

"That's just Justin being Justin."

Olivia shook her head. "I don't think so."

I opened one of Olivia's books. "Did you come here for tutoring or to talk about Justin?" The last thing I needed was someone getting my hopes up about something that wasn't going to happen.

At the end of the day it was Justin who came to look for me. I was bent over trying to retrieve my bag and didn't even hear him come in. It wasn't until he spoke that I knew he was in the room with me.

"You're not running out of here until we finish the conversation from this morning."

I placed my bag down on the desk. "I'm actually glad you came back."

Justin sat in an empty chair and pulled out the one next to him. "Can you sit beside me?"

I did as he asked. We both started to talk at the same time.

"You go first."

"No, you," he said.

"Fine." I wasn't sure where to start. "You have to realize I'm not really the type of girl who goes around asking guys out. In fact, you're the first guy I ever asked to go on a date with me. So when you said no…"

"Wait a minute," Justin jumped in. "I never said no."

"Okay, so you didn't come right out and say no, but you did say you just wanted to be friends."

"You don't get it at all."

"Hey, you wanted me to go first, so let me finish saying what I want to say."

"Fine." Justin held his hands up in surrender. "Go ahead."

"Anyway, like I was saying. I'm not really used to rejection, so I got upset. I figured you thought I wasn't good enough for you."

"What?" Justin shook his head and looked at me like he was confused.

"But then something Olivia said this morning made me realize something."

"What did she say?"

"That you were cute for a white boy." Justin looked even more confused. "It's just that everyone likes you, all the kids you coach, crazy Don, Mrs. Connor. And it's because you're nice, and there aren't enough nice people in this world. So if it's okay with you I'd like it if we could at least still be friends like you said. I know Brooklyn's a kind of long ride from where you live, but maybe we could meet somewhere halfway and hang out sometimes over the weekend. As friends. I promise I won't ask you out again."

"Really?"

"Yes, really."

Justin got up from his chair and started pacing nervously. "See, the thing is," he finally said. "When you asked me out, I didn't actually say no. I wouldn't, because the truth is I've wanted to ask you out since the first day we met, but I just didn't have the balls to do it."

That wasn't what I expected him to say. My heart started fluttering wildly in my chest, like a hummingbird's wings, and for a second I wondered if I'd heard him right.

"And then you asked me out the other day in my office, and it was after you found out about my legs, and I was sure you were only asking because you knew how much I liked you, and you thought asking me out would make me feel better."

"Oh my God, no. I wouldn't do that."

"That's what Mrs. Connor said."

"Wait. You told her?"

Justin stopped pacing and turned to look at me. "I kinda did. I'm sorry. But she knew something happened between us and she kept asking. Are you mad?"

"No, it's fine." I stood up and walked over to where Justin was and reached for one of his hands. For some reason he wouldn't look me in the eyes. I lifted his chin and locked his gaze with mine. "Hey. What's wrong?"

"Oh, Jess. I'm no good for you." I took his other hand and held them both. Justin moved closer to me and his forehead came to rest on mine. I reached out and touched his cheek. He was standing so close that I could feel the heat from his body. Between that and the way my heart was beating away in my chest I felt dizzy, drunk. Before I knew what I was doing I reached behind the nape of his neck and pulled his lips towards mine. They were softer than I imagined they'd be. I felt like I was melting into him. Our lips parted and I tasted him. He ran his hands through my hair and I felt his body quiver ever so slightly. I pulled him closer and then all of a sudden he just stopped. His lips left mine, and he stared into my eyes.

"Please don't do that again."

That was the last thing I expected him to say. I stared at him in shocked silence. "You didn't like kissing me?" I knew enough about men to know he had been really into that kiss, at least at first.

"No, no, no. That's not it."

"Then what?"

"I liked it too much," Justin said. "So much that I want to do it again and again, but I can't. You deserve someone whole."

"Is this because of your legs?" I asked. "You're turning me down because of that?"

"I'm not turning you down. At least that's not the way I see it. I'm telling you that I'm not the right guy for you. I want to be, badly, but I'm not."

"Shouldn't that be my decision to make?" I didn't get what Justin was telling me. It made no sense.

Justin leaned on the edge of the desk behind him. "All summer I've been working up the nerve to ask you out, but I just couldn't do it. And then I got an infection in one of my legs and I couldn't use my prosthetics and I was stuck at home and the whole time I was thinking about you, and then you showed up. That look on your face…"

"I told you, I was just surprised, that's all."

"Jess, even with the prosthetics I can't do things that normal people can. I can't jump into a pool on a moment's notice or dangle my feet in a stream."

"How many streams are there in New York City, Justin?"

"You're not getting my point. Sometimes I'm still in pain. I don't sleep well most nights unless I take medication. I have flashbacks, which means no war movies for me. My parents have to be careful about what they watch on TV when I'm around. I'm messed up, Jess. You deserve someone that can give you a perfect life, and I can't do that."

"It's not like I'm asking for your hand in marriage. I just wanted to go to the movies and maybe dinner."

"And then what? I'm not the kind of guy that starts something with a girl unless I think it's going to go somewhere, and I don't think you are either."

"You're overthinking this. We can start out slowly, see where things go."

"And then one day you'll decide that it's too much. That you don't want a guy with two missing legs and all the rest of my baggage."

"Is that really the kind of person you think I am?" I waited for Justin to respond, but he didn't. "I have a lot of baggage, too, you know."

"A relationship with me wouldn't be the same as one you would have with someone who isn't handicapped the way I am. You'll feel tied to me because of guilt. You won't want to hurt me by telling me that it's too much. You'll stay with me because you feel like you have to. I'm not going to let you do that to yourself. You deserve better."

"Wow. You've got this whole thing figured out, don't you?"

"What's that supposed to mean?"

"I'm just saying that you can't know that it's going to happen like that. Maybe you're going to be the one who breaks my heart. Maybe you're going to decide you don't want to date a girl like me."

Justin laughed. "I doubt there's a man out there that wouldn't want to date a girl like you."

"You don't."

"Jess, you deserve someone better than me."

"So what are you saying exactly because I feel like we're going around in circles?"

"That if your offer of friendship is still on the table, I'll take it."

I bit down on my lower lip hard and fought back against the frustration I felt start to build. It was hard to be angry when I could tell how torn up Justin was. I wanted to argue with him, convince him that I didn't care about his legs, but I could tell his mind was made up. He'd made things so impossible for me. Now that I knew he had feelings for me it would make being around him that much harder. I didn't think I could do it.

"I don't know," I said, shaking my head. I picked up my bag from the desk and started to walk away. It felt like there were no more words left to say. Nothing made sense. Justin called my name, but I kept walking. The whole way home I tried making sense out of my conversation with Justin. He didn't want to date me because he thought I deserved someone who didn't come with the kind of baggage he had. But did that mean he never intended to get involved with anyone? I didn't see how that was possible, was he just going to give up on the idea of falling in love one day? Or was it just me he couldn't get close to? By the time I made it home I hadn't come up with any answers that made sense, but I did have two text messages from Justin.

Please call me

I replied - *Can't, at a friend's and its loud here*

Talking to Justin was something I couldn't bring myself to do at that moment. I just didn't want to get back on the rollercoaster anymore.

Chapter 10

My brother arrived home an hour after I did, which was weird because he hardly ever came home on Friday nights, and when he did Mel was usually with him.

"What are you doing here?" I asked as he walked inside.

"Just came by to take a shower." He headed in the direction of the bathroom and then stopped to turn around and ask, "Mel and I are going out for drinks. Wanna come?"

"Yes!"

My bother gave me an inquisitive look. He probably hadn't expected such an animated response from me, but going out for drinks was the perfect distraction I needed to take my mind off Justin.

While my brother showered I went to look through my closet for something to wear. I chose a red silky top and a short denim skirt. Sexy, but not overly so. I was in the mood for some attention since Justin's rejection had managed to tank my ego, but I didn't want to spend the night swatting hands away from my ass.

The bar was in the city so we took the train to get there. We met Mel in front. It wasn't a place I'd ever been to before and I crossed my fingers that no one would ID me. Usually I had no trouble getting into places. Luckily, my brother knew one of the bouncers in the front and he waved us through. The bar was crowded and the music was thumping. Mel, my brother and I were able to find a table. The music was loud so I shouted across the table.

"I'm going to get a drink, any of you want anything."

"Don't worry about us," my brother said. "I was going to order some drinks in a few minutes, but you go ahead."

I scooted out of my chair and found a seat around the bar. I sat there wondering what I was in the mood for when a drink was placed in front of me. The bartender pointed to some guy sitting a few feet away. He smiled and waved. In the dim lighting of the bar it was hard to see him well, but he looked kind of cute, not really my type, but still cute. I took a sip of the drink. Long Island iced tea. Which meant he was probably trying to get me drunk. That didn't bother me, I knew how to handle myself. The guy who bought me the drink got up and walked over to me. He stuck his hand out and I shook it.

"My name's Brian," he shouted into my ear.

"I'm Jessica."

"It's nice to meet you. I saw you when you came in. For a second I thought that guy you were with was your boyfriend."

"He's my brother."

"Oh, perfect."

I sipped my drink while looking at Brian out of the corner of my eye. He kept sweeping back his hair from his forehead like he was nervous, which for some reason made me feel like laughing.

"You live around here?" he asked, leaning in again so that I could hear him. He smelled good. A lot of guys overdid it when it came to cologne, but his was just right.

"No. In Brooklyn."

"Cool," he said. "You want to get a table?"

"Ok."

Brian took my hand and led me to an empty table. After I finished my drink he ordered another. I was already starting to feel tipsy, with Long Island iced teas it didn't take many to get me there, but I didn't care. Brian was keeping my mind off Justin and helping repair my broken ego. Maybe Justin wasn't interested in me, but Brian definitely was. The drunker the two of us got, the more forward Brian became. First it was brushing my hair back over my shoulder. Then he moved closer to me and put his arm over my shoulder. Finally he moved in for a kiss. I kissed him back, but his lips weren't soft like Justin's. His kiss was rough and strange and didn't make me feel even a fraction of what I had when I'd kissed Justin only a few hours before. Even in my drunken haze it felt wrong, like I was cheating on Justin, which was stupid because he wasn't my boyfriend. He'd never be my boyfriend. The weight of my thoughts came crashing down on me, and I pulled away from Brian.

"I need to go find my brother."

Brian looked surprised. "Oh, okay. You're coming back though, right?"

"Yeah," I said, even though it was a lie. I got up and made my way to the table where Mel and my brother were sitting.

"I'm going home," I shouted to my brother.

"You sure? You and skater boy over there looked pretty cozy."

I scowled at my brother. "Yeah, I'm sure. I'll see you whenever."

I made my way outside without Brian noticing and headed for the nearest train station. That was one thing I loved about New York. You could get anywhere at any time of the day. There was no need to worry about a designated driver. Riding the train home at practically midnight and half-drunk might've seemed crazy to some people, but I'd learned how to take care of myself. That's what happened when your parents decided to dump you before you even started high school. Sink or swim, and I was one of the best swimmers I knew.

I hadn't been able to drink enough to wash away the sting of Justin's rejection. The words *not good enough* rang in my head as I rode the train home. Of course I wasn't. I had never been good enough. If I had been, my life would've been so different. I wouldn't have spent my teenage years sleeping with one eye open just in case some girl I'd managed to piss off in the group home made good on a threat to chop my hair off in my sleep. Nobody deserved to live like that, but I had, and instead of the alcohol making me forget, it was making me think about things I tried very hard to bury.

When I got off at my stop and climbed the steps out of the train station I retrieved my phone from my purse and dialed Justin's number. I was just drunk enough that my common sense didn't stop me. He answered on the first ring.

"I was hoping you'd call."

I laughed, and knew I sounded like a drunken fool.

"You okay?"

"Me? I'm more than okay."

"Are you drunk?"

"Nooo," I said, knowing that I wasn't going to be able to fool him.

"Where are you right now?"

"On my way home."

"With who?"

"With me."

"Are you crazy? You're walking home alone at night and you're drunk?"

"First of all, I'm a big girl, and I can take care of myself."

"But, your neighborhood."

"Oh yeah, that's right. It is kind of a ghetto," I said mockingly.

"That's not what I meant."

"I didn't call you so you could act like my father. I had one of those already, and I'm not looking for another."

"Then why did you call?"

"To tell you okay. If you want to be friends, then that's what we'll be…friends."

"Jess…"

"Jessica, my name's Jessica. That's what my friends call me." I hung up before Justin could get in another word. I felt like an idiot. Why the hell had I just called him? I usually was smarter than that, even after a few drinks.

Justin called back, but I didn't answer. By the time I made it inside my apartment he'd called me three more times. When I didn't answer, he texted.

Just text me when you get home, so I know you're okay.

A part of me didn't want to. I wanted him to worry. But the more reasonable side of me was starting to come back as the Long Island iced teas wore off.

I'm home, see you Monday.

I woke up with another wicked headache. That was the second time in a week I'd gotten drunk, and I felt kind of crummy about it. I also felt crummy about kissing a total stranger. After finally dragging myself out of bed and into the shower, I ate a piece of toast and headed to the laundromat where I spent most of the rest of the morning. With classes starting in another few weeks I'd need books, so I took a walk over to my university bookstore to find what I'd need for the fall semester. Between waking up late, spending my morning doing laundry and the forty minute one-way walk to the bookstore, by the time I got home later, most of Saturday was already gone.

The weekend flew by, and before I knew it, I was already back at work. I greeted Justin in the hallway on my way in, but didn't stop to talk. He found me in the break room during lunch and sat beside me as I ate.

"So you want to tell me how you came to be walking home alone at night while you were drunk?"

"Didn't I tell you I don't need a father?" This was not the conversation I was in the mood to be having. It was his fault in the first place, but I could hardly tell him that without sounding like a pathetic loser.

"I'm not trying to be your father."

"If you must know, I went out for drinks with my brother."

"Wait a minute. You're not even twenty-one, that's totally illegal. And your brother is okay with this?"

"Are you serious? You're not actually trying to tell me you never had a drink until you were twenty-one, are you?"

"No, but..."

"And as for my brother, he isn't a judgmental person." I shrugged my shoulders. "If it makes me happy, he doesn't care what I do."

"Aren't bartenders supposed to be asking for ID?"

There was no way Justin could be that clueless. "Maybe you don't find me attractive, but plenty of other people do." I regretted saying those words the minute they came out. I was trying to get a rise out of Justin—it looked like my plan was working, but I felt bad about it.

"First of all, you know perfectly well I find you attractive," Justin said, his voice controlled. "And second of all, do you really think it's a good idea letting strangers buy you drinks? What if someone tried to slip something in your drink?"

"You must think I'm stupid or something. I know better than to take my eyes off my drink."

"I guess you have an answer for everything," Justin said. "But can you do me a favor then?"

"What's that?"

"If you decide to go out drinking and walking the streets at night alone, don't call me."

"That doesn't sound like a very friendly thing to say, *friend.*"

Justin reached for my wrist and held it firmly. I looked into his eyes, he was staring at me intently. "I was half out of my mind with worry. What if someone mugged you, or tried to rape you?"

"I already told you I know how to take care of myself."

"You can tell me that a hundred times, it won't stop me from worrying. So if you don't want me getting in a cab and searching the streets of Brooklyn for you, don't call, because next time you do, I *will* come looking for you."

Justin had managed to make me feel guilty, and irritated. I felt bad that I'd made him worry, and angry because if he really cared that much then why wouldn't he change his mind about the two of us being together.

"Why do you care what I do?"

"Because…"

"That's right," I said, cutting him off. "Because we're *friends.*" The word friends sounded like it was something awful as it rolled off my tongue.

"Jess, c'mon."

"Fine. No more drunk calls, I promise." I freed myself form his grasp and stood up. "I gotta get back to work.

I could feel Justin's eyes on me as I walked away and turned to get one last quick look at him. He looked sad, and for a moment I was tempted to run back over to him and ask him what I could do, but I knew better. He was always at his most guarded when he had that look in his eyes.

As the days passed an uneasy sadness settled over me. I woke up in the mornings with a heavy feeling in my chest that didn't really go away until I was well into my workday. I was going to miss my work at the community center and the friends I made there. Even Don, who I still sometimes caught sneaking looks at my ass when I walked by him. I kept telling myself that when classes started again I'd be too busy to miss anyone, but by the time my last day at work rolled around, I still hadn't convinced myself.

I woke up early to give myself a few extra minutes to dress up. I rummaged through my closet finally settling on a peach-colored dress with white dots that cinched at my waist. After taming my hair, I put on a little extra makeup, some eyeliner and shadow instead of sticking with my usual lip gloss only look.

I felt weird as I arrived at work, like it wasn't really my last day. As usual I was greeted by Don who lifted his head from a magazine as I passed his desk.

"You look real nice."

"Thanks," I replied before heading to my classroom. I tutored three students in the morning. My last one was Linnea, who, coincidentally, had also been the first student I tutored when I started the job in June. Before we were done I jotted my number down on a piece of paper.

"Look, if you need anything, a letter of recommendation, some more help with math, just call me, okay?"

Linnea stared at me for a second and then threw her arms around me. "I'm gonna miss you, Ms. Jesse."

"I'm gonna miss you, too."

I wiped back a tear as Linnea left. I liked every kid I met over the summer, but Linnea had become special to me.

By the end of the day I was in a dark mood. I knew I should go and look for Justin and say good-bye, but I didn't think I could handle it without crying and making a total fool out of myself. Deep in thought I didn't even notice when Don poked his head into my room.

"Jessica, Mrs. Connor asked me to tell you that she wants to see you in the break room before you leave."

"Ok. I'll be there in a few minutes."

I retrieved my purse from my desk drawer and went to look for Mrs. Connor. The door to the break room was closed. I knocked and then pushed it open. To my surprise, the room was covered in streamers and balloons and besides Mrs. Connor, Justin and Don were there along with a few other community center staff and students.

"What's all this?" I asked turning a bright shade of pink.

"We wanted to throw you a good-bye party," Mrs. Connor said. She walked up to me and gave me a hug and I almost started to cry.

"We need some music up in here," Don said and went over to the radio.

One by one people walked up to me and gave me hugs and wished me well. Mrs. Connor had ordered pizzas and also bought a cake and, before I knew it, I was having too much fun to be sad. After telling jokes and eating and telling more jokes, one by one people began excusing themselves until only Justin and I were left.

He pulled something from his pocket. "I have something for you."

"What is it?"

"A good luck present."

"You mean a good-bye present?"

"No," he said softly. "Because I'm really hoping we'll see each other all the time."

"What did you get me?" I asked, steering the conversation in a different direction.

Justin handed me a small black velvet box that I was pretty sure meant jewelry. Curious, I opened it. It was a necklace. I gently lifted it out of the box and held it up for a better look. It was a thin platinum chain with three small blue jewels that dangled from little balls that matched the chain. It was beautiful and perfectly elegant.

"Did you know blue was my favorite color?"

"Of course I did. I remember everything you've told me about yourself."

"Justin." I put the necklace back in the box, closed it and held it out to him. "I can't accept a gift like this, it's too much."

"I want you to have it."

I loved the necklace, but I didn't think I could bring myself to wear it. It would remind me of Justin and what might have been if only he'd had enough faith in me and in himself.

"I'll be scared riding the train home wearing it. What if someone tries to snatch it off my neck?"

"Then put it in your purse and wear it whenever you want. You don't need to put it on now."

I hesitated for a moment before putting the box in my bag. I looked up at Justin. "Thanks. It's really beautiful," I said, trying to sound upbeat even though the same sadness I woke up with was creeping back. I pulled my bag onto my shoulder. "Well, I guess I'll see you around." *Or not.*

I turned to leave. There were a million things I wanted to say to Justin, but without a guarantee that he'd respond the way I wanted him too, I was too afraid.

"Jess."

"Yes?" I was almost at the door.

Justin hopped up on the table behind him and rested his feet on a chair. I waited for him to talk. "I'm scared," he finally said.

"Scared of what?"

"That you'll break me."

I walked over to Justin slowly and stood in front of him. "You don't believe I care about you?"

"I do. But feelings change, people change."

"I don't know what I'm supposed to be saying right now. I was the one who asked you out. I was the one who told you I was interested, but you turned me down, *twice*."

"Because I'm an idiot."

"Justin…"

"Just hear me out, okay?"

"Okay." I took a step closer to him and he reached for my hand.

"All this week I kept thinking that soon I wouldn't get to see you almost every day like I have all summer, and I couldn't stand it. When you asked me out I wanted to say yes more than anything, but by the time I realized you were actually serious and not just asking out of pity I'd had too much time to think about all the 'what ifs.' Like what if you saw my legs again and felt disgusted, or what if something happened and I was stuck in a wheelchair again? How would you handle that? Would you feel like it wasn't fair that you were stuck with me? But life is all about taking chances, and if you still want to I'm hoping that you'll let me take you out for a movie and dinner."

"I want to," I replied without hesitating.

"Come here." Justin pulled me closer and wrapped his arms around me which was a good thing because my legs were starting to feel like jelly. Justin's hand smoothed the back of my hair as he pulled me tightly to him. "You smell so good."

Justin did too, but I was too tongue tied to say anything. After another minute Justin pulled his arms back and looked into my eyes. "Do you have plans for tomorrow night?"

"No," I said, shaking my head.

"Then can I take you to a movie?"

"Tomorrow? Hmm, let me think," I teased. "Yup, that works for me."

"When you decide what you want to see, call me and I'll meet you at your house."

"You don't have to…"

Justin held a finger to my lips. "I know I don't have to, but I want to. It's a date and I'm doing it the right way. I'll meet you at your house, and we'll go to the movies together, and after to dinner, and then I'll bring you back home."

It all felt too good to be true—everything—the party, Justin's gift, him changing his mind about dating me. My commute back home seemed to last minutes instead of over an hour. All I could think about was Justin and the crazy way he made me feel when he had his arms around me.

I had to share my news with someone, I felt like I would burst if I didn't tell anyone. Since my brother wasn't home, I called Susan.

"Guess who's going on a date tomorrow?"

"With who?"

"Justin."

"Oh my God," Susan squealed into the phone. "So who asked who out this time?"

"He asked me. The staff at the community center threw me a going away party and after it was done he told me he realized he'd miss me, and that's when he asked."

"So when are you guys going out?"

"Tomorrow, he's taking me to the movies and dinner."

I knew I sounded like I was still in high school and going on a date for the first time, but I didn't care. It's how Justin made me feel, and even if I wanted to sound cool and aloof, when it came to him, I didn't think I could.

Chapter 11

Getting ready for my date with Justin seemed to consume most of my Saturday afternoon. After I got home from doing laundry, I took a shower and then carefully went through my closet trying to search for something to wear. Eventually I chose a short black skirt that was kind of velvety and paired it with a red top. People always told me I looked good in red, and I hoped Justin would agree when he saw me later. Earlier I'd called Justin to tell him what movie we were going to see. I wasn't sure what to pick. Romance was a no-no for a first date, too awkward, and I remembered what Justin said about war movies, and I sort of figured that rule applied to any movie with guns and shooting, so action was out. Luckily, there was a comedy that looked like it was going to be good.

At four, Justin arrived and I met him outside. Because it was a Saturday night, the movie theater was crowded.

"Do you mind if we sit towards the back?" Justin asked.

"No. I don't mind."

As the movie started, Justin reached for my hand. He held it while we watched the movie. I kept wondering if he was going to do anything else, which made it impossible to pay attention to the movie. That didn't matter to me, though, I still couldn't get over the fact that I was actually on a date with Justin—that I was sitting next to him in a movie theater, and he was holding my hand.

"You don't mind if I decide on where to go for dinner?" Justin asked as we exited the theater later.

"Wherever you want to go is fine with me."

Justin took my hand and we stood by the curb while he hailed a taxi. It took us to an Italian restaurant in the village. I tried to act cool as we walked inside and not make it too obvious that it was probably one of the fanciest places I'd ever been to. The truth was, I hadn't had too many opportunities for fancy in my life.

Justin and I were seated at a table in the corner of the restaurant and given menus by our host. I scanned the menu nervously trying not to gape at the fact that an order of grilled fish cost over thirty dollars.

"Just pick whatever you like," Justin said noticing my discomfort. He'd gotten good at reading me.

Our waiter approached just as I settled on the tortellini. After our orders were taken, the waiter tucked our menus under his arm and walked away leaving Justin and me alone in the corner of the restaurant.

"This place is really nice," I commented.

"It's my dad's favorite."

"Do your parents know you're out on a date tonight?" I asked. I reached for my water glass and wrapped my hands around it letting the coolness of the water slick away the sweat from my palms.

"I told my dad I was going on a date, and knowing him, that means my mom knows, too," Justin said. He took a sip of water. "What about your brother, does he know you're on a date?"

"No, but that's just 'cause I haven't seen him since yesterday morning."

"And you're not worried?"

"He spends most weekends at his girlfriend's house."

"Are the two of you close? You must be if you share an apartment."

I shrugged my shoulders. "Yes and no. My parents had sort of a divide and conquer mentality when it came to raising us. By the time the two of us left home we practically hated each other, but we got closer after."

"Really? How?"

"It's a long story."

Justin gave me a look that said *not again.* For some reason it made me smile. I supposed if we were dating I'd need to get over myself and start opening up to him. "I still want to hear it."

"I didn't see my brother for like two years after the two of us left home. Then one day it just dawned on me that he was the only family I had in New York, and we lived so close, and we hadn't seen each other in years, and something about that felt really wrong. So I called him one day and we started hanging out every now and then," I explained.

"Okay, let me get this straight. If you guys weren't living together back then, who did you live with?"

I almost forgot I hadn't told Justin about that part of my life. "Umm, well. Basically, before I went to college, I lived in a group home."

"Really?" Justin's eyes widened in disbelief. I knew he was familiar with what a group home was, several of the kids who came to the community center lived in one. "Wow. So your parents moved to Croatia when you were only fourteen, and left you behind to be cared for by the state? That's awful. I can't believe they'd do that to you."

"Well, believe it, 'cause it's true."

"But why?"

"It's hard to explain my parents. My dad was in the military when he was younger and my mom said something happened to him that messed with his head. He had a bad temper and would go off on someone at the drop of a hat. Especially me and my brother and my mom," I said. "Anyway, one day he got angry with me when one of my friends was visiting. Her mom had just come to pick her up and my father started screaming at me. He pushed me and I fell down on the steps in our house. When my friend's mother said something to him about it he went off. He started calling us all whores and told my friend that she wasn't allowed to step foot in his house again. Half an hour later the police showed up. Then a few weeks later OCFS came. My dad wouldn't let them in the house, but he told them if they wanted his kids to take them, so they did. Mike was already eighteen so he moved in with a friend and I went to a group home."

"Oh my God," Justin said. He reached for my hand and I was happy to let him hold it. It was never easy to talk about my father.

Out of the corner of my eye I spotted our waiter bringing our dinner to the table. After he set our plates down in front of us I took a bite of my pasta and gulped down some water. I knew more questions were coming.

"What about your mother?" Justin asked. It was the question I always got after I told anyone about my life. "She couldn't have been okay with your dad handing you over to the state."

"I don't know if she was okay with it or not, but she never tried to stop him. She never tried to stop any of the things my dad did. She only made excuses for him."

Pity filled Justin's eyes. Even in the dimly-lit restaurant I could see it. I tried not to let it bother me, I could hardly expect him not to react to the story I'd just told him, but I hated when people felt sorry for me.

"So you lived in the group home until you were eighteen?"

"Almost eighteen," I said between bites of my dinner. "I left when I started college and moved into the dorms. My birthday's at the end of September."

"Wow. That makes me feel lucky to have the parents I do."

"You should feel lucky." I didn't know that much about Justin's parents, but I knew they were better than mine. Most people's were. They came through for Justin after he got hurt, when he really needed them. If I got injured the way Justin had, I doubt my parents would've lifted a finger for me.

"My parents are really nice, but sometimes I can't help but feel like they're disappointed in me."

"Disappointed in you? How is that even possible?"

Justin frowned. "My parents were *really* unhappy about my choice to join the Navy. They wanted me to go to college, but it wasn't what *I* wanted. My dad tried to convince me to at least get a degree first and join the military as an officer, but I didn't listen to him. I've always known I wasn't really a desk job sort of guy, I wanted to see the world, I wanted adventure, not some boring job as an investment banker—that's what my parents both do in case you were wondering."

"I don't see you as an investment banker."

"Because it's not me," Justin said. "But the military thing didn't really work out either. Once you lose your legs, that's it, you're out. I got medically discharged after being in for less than five years. My parents flew straight out to the hospital after they heard about my injury, they hired the best therapists money could buy, even though the military pays for your medical expenses. I don't think I could have gone through all the agony of having my legs amputated and learning to walk all over again without them. But sometimes when they look at me I feel like I can hear them thinking that if I'd only listened to them I'd still have my legs."

"I'm sorry." I wanted to say something more powerful than that, but I couldn't think of what.

Justin shrugged. "Don't be. What's done is done. If I spend too much time thinking about it I find myself in a really dark place. I don't want to go there, especially not tonight." Justin reached for my hand again like he had earlier. "Are you having a good time tonight?"

"The best."

"Are you sure?"

"Yes, I'm sure." It was crazy to me the way Justin doubted himself. He didn't see himself the way I saw him, that was for sure.

"Should we order dessert?"

"I don't think I could stuff another bite into my belly right now."

"Then how about just ordering something for later." Justin searched for our waiter, then raised his hand to get his attention. "Can we look at the dessert menu?"

Justin insisted on sending me home with not one but two desserts. "If you don't want it, maybe your brother will."

"If you're trying to get my brother to like you by buying him food you should know you really don't need to go to the trouble," I joked. "My brother pretty much likes everyone."

"Actually, the only person I'm worried about getting to like me right now is you," Justin said as he finished paying for our meal.

"You already know you don't need to worry about that."

Alone with him in the taxi on our way back to Brooklyn I secretly prayed for us to get stuck in traffic so I could have more time with him. His arm went around my back and he pulled me closer to him. Even in the dim light I could see his eyes sparkle as the street lights reflected in them. Heat radiated off his body, I felt flushed. I wanted him to lean down and kiss me and then…he did. I reached around his neck, drawing him closer to me. His tongue parted my lips, searching. Our bodies twisted towards each other. Justin's hands stroked the sides of my face and neck as he kept his lips on mine kissing me in a way I would have sworn I'd never been kissed before. I could feel Justin's desire, but there was more to our kiss than that, it was tender in a way I hadn't experienced before.

"You don't know how badly I wanted to do that again."

I bit my lower lip still hoping I could taste him and to keep myself from smiling the goofy smile I felt coming on.

Justin wrapped his arms around me. "I wish we could go

somewhere private, somewhere where it was just the two of us."

"Well I'd invite you over, but knowing my luck my brother will be back home." That was an excuse. I was pretty sure my brother would be gone all weekend. Justin had already seen my apartment once, but things were different then. I felt self-conscious about bringing him back there now.

"That's okay. It's probably for the best we don't rush things anyway."

I wasn't sure exactly what he meant by that, but I didn't ask. Instead I kissed him again and again and before I knew it the taxi had pulled up in front of my apartment and I had to say goodnight.

I walked inside my dump of an apartment with only my cat to keep me company, but it didn't matter. I felt on top of the world anyway.

Chapter 12

Justin and I talked on the phone every night. Sometimes just for a few minutes, and other times we talked late into the night about silly things, like our favorite things to eat, what we liked to do, what our favorite colors were. Even after hours on the phone I hated saying goodnight.

I looked forward to weekends in a way I never had before. Justin had the idea to pretend we were tourists and go to places we'd both been to a million times before like the Empire State Building, Liberty Island, and Chinatown. Everything seemed new when I did it with Justin, like I was seeing something for the first time. In the evenings we went to dinner. Justin took me to the fanciest places, even though I insisted I was perfectly happy with pizza.

"I'm going to get fat with all these fancy restaurants you keep bringing me to," I teased.

"You'll still be beautiful to me." Justin seemed to always know the perfectly right things to say.

"So, a little birdie told me your birthday was coming up in a few weeks," Justin said one afternoon as we walked through Washington Square Park.

"Oh really? Which birdie was this?"

I knew perfectly well who it was. My brother, who had an uncanny ability to make friends with anyone, was home one afternoon when Justin came to pick me up and answered the door before I could get to it. The two of them chatted while I finished getting ready in my room and I was pretty sure I overheard Mike mentioning my birthday.

"Does it matter?"

"No, not really."

"So what do you want to do for it?"

"It's just a birthday. I don't want to make a big deal out of it."

"Well, that's too bad, because I've been racking my brain trying to decide how to make it really special for you."

"C'mon. You know you don't have to do that."

"My girl only turns twenty once," Justin said. "We're going to celebrate it."

It was an unusually warm September day and as we walked, I noticed Justin seemed uncomfortable. I wondered if it was the heat. Hot weather, it turned out, was the enemy of an amputee who wore prosthetics.

"C'mon. Let's sit," I said, pulling him towards a bench. Justin didn't seem any more comfortable seated than when we were walking. "Why is it that you never wear shorts?"

Justin looked at me funny. "Are you kidding me?"

"What? It's got to be more comfortable than wearing pants in this heat."

"I'd rather deal with the heat than have a bunch of people staring at my cyborg legs all day."

"Your cyborg legs? Is that what you call them?" I realized then that I had never seen Justin's prosthetics.

He shrugged. "My brother Jeff started calling them that, and it just sort of stuck."

"Is that really what happens? People stare at you?"

"I wouldn't know. I've always worn pants since I started using the prosthetics. Before that I used my wheelchair, and yes, people stared and strangers asked questions all the time. I *hated* it."

I felt bad for even mentioning the whole shorts thing. We sat beside each other in silence for a few minutes. I struggled to think of something right to say. Finally Justin broke the silence.

"So, I sort of had this idea," he said. "But I don't want you to get the wrong idea."

"Get the wrong idea about what?"

Justin tucked some of my hair behind my ear. "We're always saying that we wished we could have some time alone, just the two of us."

"Yes, I think I remember saying that a few times." I smiled. I'd said it more than a few times. In fact, it was something I mentioned on every date because kissing in a dark movie theater or in the back of a taxi wasn't exactly ideal. But since I lived in a tiny, not very private apartment with my brother, and Justin lived with his parents, our choices were limited.

"I was thinking that we could maybe get a hotel room together for your birthday weekend."

I stared at Justin not really knowing how to respond. It wasn't what I'd expected him to say, even though it was probably the most perfect idea I'd heard in a long time. Justin looked away, like he was embarrassed. "I'm sorry, I didn't mean to assume..."

"Hey." I reached for his chin and made him turn around and look at me. "I'd love to spend a whole weekend with you."

"We don't have to…you know, if you don't want to. I just want to spend time with you."

I tried to keep from laughing. "I wasn't thinking you were trying to get me into bed," I said.

It was the first time I'd seen him blush. "You're sure about this?" he asked after he regained his composure.

"Very."

The next two weeks seemed to crawl by. I was seriously nervous and excited at the same time. Even though Justin said he wasn't trying to get me into bed I decided that just in case it happened I should be prepared. I was already on the pill, I had been for years, just to keep my periods regular, but I also bought a box of condoms. A few days before my birthday I went shopping for some nice underwear. My heart fluttered in my chest as I pictured myself wearing them for Justin. It had been a really long time since I'd been with a guy, and the thought of it made me blush.

As my birthday weekend approached, I made sure to get as much school work and studying in as I could, since I didn't want to have to worry about it over the weekend. I did laundry Friday after my last class, packed a small overnight bag, fed Buddy and waited for Justin to pick me up. It was almost seven when he finally arrived. His hair was freshly cut and he was wearing a pair of dark jeans and a thin tawny colored sweater that hugged his chest and brought out the gold flecks in his brown eyes.

I ran outside with my bag over my shoulder and jumped into his arms.

"Whoa."

"Sorry, I'm just excited," I said. "I didn't mean to almost knock you over."

"Then, let's go." Justin held out his hand, I took it and followed him inside the cab. Our hotel was close to Central Park and the most modern, elegant place I'd ever stepped foot into. The view from our room was magnificent. I stood by the window staring out at the park nearby. Justin circled his arms around me from behind.

"Do you like it?"

"It's amazing." I turned my head to look at him. "Can you believe this view?"

Justin kissed the side of my head. "It's the most spectacular view on the planet," he said.

He wasn't even looking outside. "I meant the view out there."

"It's hard for me to look at anything else when you're around."

"Oh, that's a good one," I teased.

"How about some dinner? It's after seven, and I know you must be hungry, so nothing too far from here. I heard the restaurant downstairs is supposed to be really good."

Really good turned out to be an understatement. The restaurant's décor was sort of art deco style decorated in shades of amber and brown, from the plush dining chairs to the light fixtures and the carpet. Huge vases filled with gigantic bouquets flanked the entrance and adorned the bar.

I ordered lamb, one of my favorite dishes, and tried not to think about later, when it would be just the two of us.

"So where did you tell your parents you were going this

weekend?" I asked, figuring they must have wondered why he wasn't going to be home for the next two nights.

"To a friend's."

"A friend? Not your girlfriend?"

"My parents know I'm dating someone, but I figured it was safer not to let them know I was going to be with you all weekend."

"What do you mean by that?"

"No one's good enough for us boys. At least not according to my mother. The questions would've never ended if I had told my mother where I was really going."

I wanted to ask Justin when he planned on letting his mother know about me. Not just that he was dating someone, but that he had a girlfriend, one he spent a lot of time with. But maybe it was too soon. After all, we'd only been dating for a month. "Doesn't your mother want you to be happy? She must want you to find someone."

He shrugged. "I don't know, sometimes I wonder if she does. A part of me thinks she's happy having me at home, and happy that I need her help the way I do."

"That doesn't seem right."

"Maybe I'm making her sound worse than she is. If it weren't for my mother I don't know how I would have survived after my injury. But almost dying scared the hell out of her. I swear she still worries about me like I'm back in Afghanistan."

Justin and I finished eating and the waiter came over with our check. Even after everything was squared away Justin didn't get up from the table. Before I had a chance to ask him what the matter was he started talking.

"So, there's something I should probably tell you now." Justin sounded really serious. That made me nervous.

"What is it?"

He shifted in his chair before answering. "I don't sleep with my prosthetics on."

It took me a second to register what he was trying to tell me. "And you're worried about what I'll think when I see your legs again?" It was practically a distant memory—the morning when I learned Justin's secret. But I hadn't seen his legs for very long that day, so I barely remembered what they looked like.

"It's not very pretty."

"I saw you without your prosthetics before," I tried reassuring him. "I was fine with it then, and I'll be fine with it later."

"There's a difference between seeing them for a few seconds and sleeping next to me all night," Justin said. He sounded sad and lost. He always did when he talked about his legs. I wished I knew exactly what to say to put his mind at ease, but the right words didn't come to me. I reached for his hand and laced my fingers through his.

"I swear it will be fine. It won't matter to me." There wasn't a doubt in my mind, but I could tell Justin was worried. "We're a couple, right, you and me?"

"I thought of you as my girl since our first date." It was funny that Justin said that. We'd never had the whole boyfriend girlfriend discussion, I just took it for granted that it was what we both wanted. Still, it felt nice to have Justin confirm it for me.

"And that means you take the good with the bad. I don't care about your legs, I just want to be with you, and I want you to trust me enough to know that."

"I'm sorry, you're right. It's just that I was so excited about the idea of spending time with you alone, that I never thought about the rest of it, but sitting here with you now, knowing that in a few minutes it'll just be the two of us, I guess I'm kind of nervous."

"Let's just go upstairs and watch a movie or something. We can pretend we're at the movies instead of in a hotel room together."

Justin laughed. "I don't think I'll be able to stretch my imagination that far, and I'm not sure I want to either." I stood and held my hand out. Justin reached for it and the two of us made our way into the elevator and back to our room.

A chilled bottle of champagne was waiting for us when we got upstairs. Justin opened it, filled two glasses and handed me one.

"I can't believe you're only turning twenty," he commented.

"Are you saying I look old?"

"No, you look beautiful. But I don't know many twenty-year-olds putting themselves through college, working, and paying their own rent, without help from anyone."

"It's not like I really had a choice. You do what you have to in life."

Justin lifted his glass. "Well, here's to you. The strongest and most beautiful woman I've ever met."

We clinked our glasses and sipped our champagne. Flattered as I was by Justin's toast, his words made me uncomfortable. I didn't think of myself as strong, just as someone who had to make do with what was handed to her. There were plenty of nights I cried myself to sleep because of the things that happened in my life. If I was really strong, I wouldn't have cried, I would have kept my chin held high and not whined about the fact that I didn't have normal parents who cared about me and wanted to help me instead of throwing me out into the world before I was done with junior high school.

Justin put his glass down on the table. "I think it's present time." He walked over to his suitcase, unzipped it and pulled out one big box and another smaller one.

"Justin, this is too much," I said as he handed me the two boxes.

"No, it's not." Justin sat down on the edge of the bed. "Go on, open them."

I hesitated before pulling the top off the bigger box. There was a hat and gloves inside in a bright cranberry red color, I pulled them out of the box and held them against my cheek. It was the softest material I had ever felt.

"It's cashmere."

"They're so soft," I said before setting them aside and lifting out a coat that had been resting under the hat and gloves. The coat was black and cinched at the waist. I tried it on and couldn't help but smile. It was beautiful, elegant. I didn't want to take it off.

"Do you like it? I wanted you to have something nice for when it gets cold."

"I love it." I took the coat off and folded it back into the box it had come in. "Thank you so much."

"You still have one more present to open."

Justin handed me the small box. I took it and opened it

slowly. It was a pair of earrings. Small platinum hoops with three tiny blue stones dangling from the bottom. They were a match to the necklace he'd bought me on my last day working at the community center.

"Justin," I said, trying to catch my breath. I felt like crying. It was too much, more than I expected, even from Justin who treated me like a princess every second the two of us were together. "They're beautiful, but you didn't have to get me all this."

"Come here, Jess."

I walked over to where Justin was sitting. He wrapped his arms around my waist and rested his head against my stomach. Then he looked up at me, got on his feet, rested his hands on my waist and kissed me softly on my lips. "I know I didn't have to, but I wanted to. I like making you happy. You're just going to have to get used to it."

"You make me happy even without the gifts."

Justin sat back down and then pulled me onto his lap. My legs straddled his waist, and I wrapped my arms around the nape of his neck and rested my forehead on his. I inhaled Justin's scent, a mix of soap and cologne, and then he kissed me on my neck just under my jawline. My body tensed, his lips felt so good on my bare skin. I moved my hands up to the back of his head. For another moment he continued to kiss my neck and then I pressed my lips to his. Knowing that it was just the two of us and that there was no chance of my brother walking in made holding back impossible. I yearned for Justin and, at the same time, I could feel his desire for me, which only made me want him more. His lips gently tugged on mine and then he parted my mouth with his tongue, kissing me like I was his air and all he needed to breathe. His lips left mine and traveled down to my neck again, every inch of my body tingled, I felt like I was being consumed. I ran my hands under his shirt overcome with the desire to feel his bare skin under my fingers.

As my fingers stroked Justin's back he let out a soft moan. I wanted him to do the same to me, to touch me the way I was touching him, instead he pulled back. "We better stop."

I wanted to ask why, but I didn't. I very much doubted that the problem was Justin not wanting me. I could feel his desire, the more we kissed the more I knew I was exciting him, so there had to be another reason he wanted to stop and I was pretty sure it had to do with his legs. We'd never talked about how it would be if we ever became intimate with each other.

"Are you okay?"

"It's just that I've never...you know, at least not since I lost my legs."

"But you can, right?"

"Oh, I can," Justin said. "It's just that, I guess I feel a little self-conscious."

"Maybe if we do something else first." I slid off Justin's lap and went to look for the remote control. "Let's just watch TV."

Justin smiled and scooted back up on the bed. I nestled beside him and started flipping through the channels until we found something both of us wanted to watch. As the minutes ticked by I kept wondering when Justin would kiss me again or even if he would.

After an hour, I got up to go to the bathroom. When I came back Justin was sitting on the edge of the bed. He'd poured us two more glasses of champagne. I only took a sip of mine because I really wasn't in the mood to drink, I was too nervous thinking about how the rest of our night would unfold. I watched Justin as he sipped his drink. Before he could finish I reached for his glass, plucked it from his hands, placed it on the nightstand and leaned down to kiss him. Apparently, I realized, I was going to have to take matters in my own hands. Hungrily I searched for his tongue as I wound my hands behind his neck and sat on his lap straddling him. His arms circled my body and, as I felt his desire for me grow, I started kissing his neck. I wanted to turn him on so badly he wouldn't be able to ask me to stop. My tongue traced every inch of his collarbone and as he moaned I reached under his shirt again. He inhaled sharply, but this time instead of stopping me he lifted his shirt over his head and tossed it on the floor.

His chest was perfectly chiseled. For months I'd imagined what he looked like without his shirt on. I ran my hands over the muscles on his chest and arms. Justin reached for the hem of my shirt and I helped him lift it over my head. I scooted off Justin's lap and gently pushed him down onto the bed. He lifted his legs from the floor and when his entire body was flat on the bed I straddled him again. Justin looked up at me and touched my breasts. My bra was still on, I wanted to feel his hands on my bare skin so I reached around my back and unhooked it letting my bra fall on the bed beside me.

"You're so beautiful," Justin said as he reached to touch me again. I moaned as his fingertips ran over my hardened nipples. I felt like I was going to explode with desire. Slowly I lowered my body until I was lying on top of Justin. The feel of his bare skin on mine made me shudder.

"Are you okay?" Justin asked.

"Very okay." I kissed him again, first on his lips, then his neck again, and then his chest. He moaned and arched his back. I reached for the button to his pants. Justin grabbed ahold of my hands.

"Are you sure?"

"Yes," I said. My heart pounded in my chest. I was nervous as hell but I wanted him, there was no doubt in my mind.

Justin pulled my skirt down to my knees, I got it off the rest of the way. From his pocket, Justin pulled out a condom. "You came prepared," I teased.

"Well, I was hoping. But if…"

"No buts. I want you. Now."

Somehow we managed to get the rest of our clothes off. The room was dark, only lit by a bedside lamp, and I didn't even glance down at Justin's legs. I didn't care about that, the only thing I cared about was being with him, touching and tasting every inch of his flesh. I stayed on top and when he finally entered me I gasped, surprised at how good it felt to have him inside me. His body rocked under mine. I arched my back as Justin's hands went to my breasts again.

"Open your eyes," Justin breathed.

I did as he asked and lowered my body forward so I could look into his eyes. Overcome with emotion I spoke without thinking. "I love you."

Justin froze under me. "You what?"

I didn't know how to answer him. I hadn't intended on letting him know. *Never tell a guy you love him first.* That was one of the rules of dating that had been passed down to me by some of the older girls I'd known when I lived in the group home.

"I said I love you," I whispered into Justin's ear. It was too late to take it back, and besides, it was true. Maybe Justin wasn't ready to tell me the same thing, maybe he never would be, but at that moment I didn't care, I just wanted him to know.

Justin eased my head up a bit and kissed me on my lips deeply, passionately, he wrapped his hands in my hair and then grabbed my bottom as the two of moved in rhythm with each other again. His hands gripped my waist and I moaned in pleasure as he led me to climax. My heart still racing and my body still on fire from the pleasure I felt from him I almost didn't notice as Justin's body tensed under mine. He gasped and pulled me down onto him, his hands wrapped in my hair again. I lay down on his chest and listened to his heart pounding. Justin turned to his side as I slid beside him. He propped himself up on one of his arms and lifted my chin with his free hand so I could look in his eyes.

"I love you, too."

I looked away from Justin. "You don't have to say that just because I did."

"That's not why I said it." I gave him a skeptical look. "I wanted to tell you first, but I was worried I'd scare you off. I just didn't think it was possible that you could love me."

"Why would you think that? You're like the perfect guy, handsome, kind, generous, what's not to love?"

"This." Justin pointed to his legs. It was the first time I'd ever seen his prosthetics. Nothing about them bothered me. The only thing that got to me was thinking about the pain losing his legs must have caused him. I'd never seen anyone wearing them in real life before, but they looked exactly like I imagined they would based on what I'd seen on television.

"Why is it so hard for you to believe that it doesn't make a difference to me?"

"That's a story for another time."

"No." I insisted. "I've told you things, plenty of things about myself. It's your turn to now."

Justin lay back down on the bed and sighed. I waited for him to start talking and explain why he was so afraid that his injury made him so impossible to love. "I was eighteen when I joined the Navy," he began. "I had a girlfriend, and before I got deployed I asked her to marry me."

My throat tightened as he mentioned another girl. She was his past, but I was still jealous. "What happened to her?"

"Let's just say that before I left for Afghanistan I had two perfect legs and a fiancée, and when I came back I had none of those things."

"She left you because of your injury?" I asked sharply. I already hated this girl for having been engaged to Justin, now I hated her more knowing that she broke his heart.

"Not at first. When I finally came back home, Erin, that was her name, seemed happy to see me and relieved that I was still alive after what had happened. But we couldn't do the things we had done before. I was still trying to learn how to walk on my new legs. I had doctor and physical therapy appointments all the time and Erin wanted to do what all twenty-two year old women want to do—have fun, go out, and party. I couldn't do any of those things."

"So she broke up with you?"

"No. I think she wanted to, but she felt guilty about it. I'm the one who broke up with her."

"Why?"

"I overheard her talking to one of her friends on her phone one day. Whoever it was must have invited her to do something because I heard her say that she couldn't because she was stuck with Stumpy."

"Oh my God. She actually used those words?" Justin nodded. I couldn't believe that Justin had ever loved someone who could be so cruel. "That's terrible."

"I tried to convince myself I hadn't heard her right, but I knew I had. She seemed almost relieved when I confronted her about it, like she was wondering how long it would take me to be the one to break it off because she couldn't handle the guilt of dumping her damaged boyfriend."

"That's why you said no, when I asked you out. You thought I felt sorry for you, you didn't believe I actually liked you for you."

Justin nodded.

"What made you change your mind?"

"A few things. Mrs. Connor for one, you for another. I just didn't see that in you. You don't have a mean bone in your body. And, well, every time I pictured you with someone else I'd lose my mind a little. I didn't just want you to be mine, I felt like I needed you to be."

"I hate to disappoint you, but I have multiple mean bones in my body."

Justin kissed my shoulder softly. "I don't believe that."

"I'm sorry you got hurt. But that girl was stupid; she didn't realize what she had."

"Losing Erin was hard. Not really because it was her; truthfully we were pretty mismatched, but because it came at the worst possible time. I'd just lost my legs, then my career in the Navy, then my fiancée. I was in a dark, dark place for a long time after that, but eventually I got over her," Justin said. He reached for my hand and twined his fingers through mine. "I don't think I could handle losing you, though. Every time I picture my future you're always there."

Justin's perfect words echoed in my mind. I tried hard not to think about how too good to be true he was. Things in my life usually had a way of not working themselves out the way I wanted them to. What I craved most seemed to have a way of slipping through my fingers. There were many times I wondered if happiness just wasn't in the cards for me. But I tried not to think that way and just let myself feel happy as I lay beside Justin.

Chapter 13

Somehow I managed to drift asleep. I woke up sometime later startled. For a minute I didn't realize where I was. I turned to look at the bedside clock. It was just after midnight. Justin was asleep beside me. I tried falling back asleep, but couldn't. I got out of bed meaning to go to the bathroom. It was then that I noticed that Justin had removed his prosthetics and placed them beside the bed.

After showering and putting on some fresh underwear and a shirt I crawled back in bed next to Justin. I wanted to see his legs again, to see what he looked like without his prosthetics, but I left the blankets in place. Justin would let me see if that's what he wanted. It didn't seem right to sneak a look while he slept. I nestled next to Justin in bed and a few minutes later he stirred.

"You're awake?" he asked.

"I took a shower."

Justin sniffed my still wet hair. "Mmmm, you smell good." He kissed the side of my head.

"Can I ask you something?"

"You want to see my legs?"

"How did you know that's what I was going to ask you?"

"I just figured."

"Does it bother you?"

"No." He pulled back the blankets and I turned on the bedside lamp. Both legs looked totally normal until you got to just below his knee. From there they tapered a bit and then just stopped.

"I'm told I was lucky. Below the knee amputations aren't as bad as above the knee, much easier to learn how to walk on prosthetics."

"It must have hurt like hell."

Justin nodded and then pulled the covers back up. "It was a nightmare. From start to finish, the day I lost my legs was the worst day of my life."

"Can you tell me what happened?"

"I was deployed with a Marine battalion in Afghanistan as one of their Corpsmen. Me and the team I was on were out on patrol one night when we stumbled on an IED. There was a huge explosion and the next thing I remember is being flat on my back and feeling the most excruciating pain in my legs. I heard screams, at first I thought they were mine, but then I realized I wasn't the only one who got hurt. A few of the Marines I was with did, too." Justin shook his head and closed his eyes for a moment before opening them again. "It was my job to help them, to save their lives, but I couldn't. One of my Marines died, another lost part of his arm while I lay there helpless."

"Justin." I couldn't believe he blamed himself for what happened. "It wasn't your fault. There was nothing you could do."

"The logical part of me knows that." Justin's voice sounded hollow, distant. "But I'll never forget that feeling. The feeling of utter failure, of knowing that people depended on me and I couldn't pull through for them."

I wrapped one of my arms around Justin and kissed his chest. "You are not a failure. It's not like you asked to be injured. If anything you're a hero."

"That's what everyone keeps telling me. I even have the Purple Heart to prove it, but the guilt never goes away. I think about that Marine who died, and sometimes I think it should have been me. For months after it happened I wished that it were."

I hated the idea of Justin lying around in a hospital in pain and wishing he were dead. "You're not the one who planted that IED. Nothing that happened that night was your fault. Bad things happen to good people all the time, and there isn't a reason for it. It just happens. For whatever reason, you made it out of there alive, and I for one am grateful you did."

"For a very long time I wished I'd died that night. At first it was because of the pain of my injury, then it was the agony of rehab and trying to learn how to walk again. And then it was just realizing that my life in the military was over, and I was a twenty-something-year-old man with no legs stuck at home with his parents and no job or any prospects of one."

"How did you wind up working at the community center then?"

"Through a program that was looking to hire vets. I used to think that job saved me, and in a lot of ways it did, but the truth is, meeting you has made me happier than I can ever remember being. Even before I lost my legs."

I was stunned speechless. "You seemed so normal when we met. I would have never guessed that you had been through what you had."

"Call it self-preservation. I learned how to cover what I was thinking and feeling," Justin explained. "Once you meet my mom you'll understand."

"What do you mean?"

"My mother's a total helicopter. She's constantly hovering over me, looking for signs that I'm cracking. I think if it was up to her I'd still be seeing some shrink every day. It drives me crazy. So, whenever I would get in a mood I'd have to find a way to hide it from her or deal with her trying to convince me that she knows what I need better than I do."

"Have you ever thought about moving out and getting your own place?"

"I've thought about it, lots of times. I just don't know if I'm ready yet. I keep thinking about all the things that could go wrong."

"I guess it would be hard to find an apartment in Manhattan for what you earn at the community center."

"My paycheck isn't that great, but I also get some money from disability, and I have money that's been left to me by family, so it's really not about the money," Justin explained. "After I got out of the hospital the therapists I was seeing said I shouldn't be on my own, that it wasn't good for me to isolate myself. But truthfully, I was actually thinking about getting my own apartment for the past few months, until I got that skin infection in my leg over the summer, and I couldn't use my prosthetics. Being stuck in a wheelchair really scared me. It's hard, you can't even imagine how difficult it is to do things when you can't stand on two legs. Everyone keeps telling me that eventually I'll be independent again, but I'm not sure I really believe it."

"Justin, if anyone can do it, you can." I didn't want to push the subject any further. It couldn't have been easy for Justin to confide in me as much as he had. Still, I felt bad hearing how little confidence he had in himself.

Justin kissed me again, pulled his arm away and sat up.

"What's wrong?"

"Just figured I'd take a shower, too." Justin pointed to his suitcase. "Do you mind bringing that over here for me?"

I got out of bed and pulled it over to him. He unzipped it and pulled out a different set of prosthetic legs than the ones that were by the bed.

"They're for showering," Justin explained. "I can't get the other ones wet."

I watched as Justin attached the legs and walked towards the bathroom. I didn't understand the way Justin saw himself. Even before he'd told me about what he'd been through I'd been in awe of his courage, and the way he picked himself up and moved on after the tragedy he'd endured. Now that I knew the whole story, I was even more impressed. As Justin showered, I lay in bed waiting for him, hoping he'd hurry, because I had the craziest urge to have him back in my arms.

A few minutes later, Justin emerged from the bathroom with a towel wrapped around his waist. I smiled as he walked over to me, thinking about what was under that towel. Justin sat on the edge of the bed and I watched as he removed his prosthetic legs without saying a word. I wondered if he felt awkward doing that around me and how long it would be before he wasn't. There had to be a first time, a first time for me to see him without his legs and then every time after would feel more and more normal until he was so comfortable around me that he never gave it another thought.

Justin sat on the edge of the bed like he was waiting for me to say or do something. I scooted closer to him and then started to kiss the droplets of water that still dotted his back and shoulders.

"Turn around," I whispered.

Justin obeyed and covered my mouth with his. He swung his body around on the bed and I lay down as he showered me with kisses. The towel that was around his waist had come undone and I flung it off the bed and reached for Justin's hardness. Justin pulled down my underwear and then lifted my shirt off.

"I want you so bad," he breathed.

I moved my legs apart. "I'm yours," I said and then Justin entered me again.

He made love to me with a hunger and urgency that he hadn't earlier that night. I moaned as Justin brought me to climax, feeling wild with pleasure.

Maybe it was the fact that we'd opened up to each other so much. Whatever bond the two of us had already started to form towards each other felt more cemented.

Chapter 14

Justin wasn't around when I woke up. I went to the bathroom to look for him, but he wasn't there. His stuff was still in the hotel room which meant he hadn't just up and left me. I reached for my phone to call him, but put it back on the nightstand without dialing his number. I didn't want him to think I was clingy and desperate. Wherever he had gone, I was sure he'd come back.

It was another fifteen minutes before I heard him fumbling at the door. I got up to help him open it. He smiled as he walked into the room.

"I got us some breakfast." Justin held up a large brown bag before putting it down on the dresser. Then he put one hand on my waist and the other around my back and pulled me towards him.

"Why didn't you leave a note? I was worried."

"You were fast asleep." Justin kissed me. "I figured I'd be back before you were up."

He stepped back from me and then pulled out four take-out boxes from the bag. "I wasn't sure what you liked for breakfast so I brought you a few things. There's eggs in there, and some pancakes in that one." Justin pointed to the boxes.

"You." I couldn't help the smile on my face. "You're always spoiling me."

"Of course. What do you expect? You're my girl."

His girl. I liked the sound of that. It made my heart leap in my chest.

We spent the rest of the day hanging out in Central Park and had an early dinner before heading back to our room. Justin had barely closed the door behind us when he pulled me into his arms. We kissed and grabbed at each other's clothes, peeling them off before making it to the bed.

"You're insatiable," I teased him afterwards.

"It's been a really long time for me."

"No one since that girl you told me about yesterday?"

"Yup. She was actually the only person I'd ever been with, until you." I didn't like the pang of envy that Justin's words brought. "What about you?"

"What about me?"

"You've never really talked about your dating past. Except for that guy you lived with before."

"I like keeping my past in the past."

"You think I'll get jealous?"

"Can we change the subject, please?" I didn't like thinking about the relationships I'd had. All of them had been disastrous in one way or another. It had taken me a long time to wise up about my life and I didn't like to reminisce about the more painful times when all I'd done was make stupid mistake after stupid mistake.

"Okay, okay. As long as you do something for me."

"What's that?"

"Kiss me again." I had no problem complying with Justin's request. That night the two of us hardly slept. Maybe it was because we knew it was the last night we'd have completely alone together for a while.

Heading back home after my weekend with Justin was harder than I imagined it would be. My brother wasn't home, he was probably with his girlfriend, and I envied him for being able to do that. Mike almost never spent a night without Melanie. Most of the time he stayed at her place, sometimes she stayed over ours, but it was different for him. Mike had the bedroom at the front of the house so there was never any reason for me to go to his room. My bedroom was sandwiched between his and the kitchen area which meant he had to walk through my room to get to the kitchen or bathroom. That was a less than ideal situation if you were interested in privacy. And even if that wasn't an issue, I still felt self-conscious about my apartment.

Over the next few weeks I threw myself into studying during the week so I wouldn't have to stress about my classwork on the weekends when I was with Justin. Midterms were coming up and I was determined to do well despite the fact that I stayed up late most nights talking to Justin on the phone. I hardly saw Susan anymore since we weren't taking any classes together. My brother I only saw briefly in passing a few times during the week. Then one random morning Mike surprised me by bringing me a cup of my favorite hazelnut flavored coffee from the deli near our apartment. I was in the kitchen eating breakfast when he strolled inside and pulled up a chair next to me.

"What's up?" I asked, figuring he had something to say to me.

"I've been thinking about asking Mel to marry me," he blurted out.

I almost dropped my cup on the floor. I knew Mike loved his girlfriend, but for whatever reason I just didn't see my brother as the marrying type.

"Are you going to say something?" he asked, as I sat there staring at him in shocked silence.

"Does Mel know?"

Mike shook his head. "No. And I don't want her to until I can get her a ring first."

"Wow! Well I won't say anything. I promise." I wondered how my brother was going to be able to buy the kind of ring Mel would be happy with. He made decent money, but engagement rings costs thousands of dollars.

"I just got a promotion at work which means more money. I think in a few months I'll have enough saved up for a ring. I was thinking about asking her on Christmas."

"Oh my God." I stood up to give Mike a hug. "I'm so excited for you."

"Thanks, J. You think Mel will say yes?"

"Of course she will."

"Well, if she does, I don't want you to worry about what's going to happen to you, okay? I know you still have a year and a half left of school."

"You don't have to put your life on hold for me." Even though I said it I only kind of meant it. If my brother moved out before I graduated and got my first real job I would be toast.

Despite how happy I was for my brother, my precarious situation consumed my thoughts over the next few weeks. Of course I knew I wouldn't *always* have my brother to rely on, but I hadn't really considered that eventually he'd want to get married and move on with his life instead of living with his little sister.

Justin kept bugging me to tell him what was on my mind, but I wouldn't. He liked to fix things and I was too proud to accept more from him than he'd already given me. At night when I was supposed to be sleeping my anxious thoughts kept me up. I worried about not finishing my classes on time and not finding a job after graduation. If any of those things happened I had no backup plan. There was no doting uncle or grandparent who would float me a loan until I got on my feet. The only family I'd ever known growing up was my brother and my parents. Every other relative was still in Croatia and it had been so long since my parents had brought me and Mike back for a visit that I barely remembered any of their names and faces.

The weather had been getting colder and colder. The leaves on the few trees that lined the streets in downtown Brooklyn turned orange and yellow and red and then fell off. The days got shorter and store shelves started to fill with boxes of stuffing and cans of pumpkin puree. I hated the holidays and tried my best to ignore that they were on their way. Holidays were for families, and every storefront held a reminder that I didn't really have one. I didn't want to be the person who dragged everyone down so I kept my feelings bottled up inside and did my best to act as if nothing bothered me.

Early one Saturday morning it was so cold in my apartment

that I refused to get out of bed. Somewhere in the back of my closet the space heater I'd been forced to buy was safe in its box, but I just couldn't drag myself out from under my pile of blankets— not until I heard someone knocking on my door.

I groaned, wrapped my blanket around myself and got up to see who it was.

"What are you doing here?" I asked shocked to see that it was Justin. I hadn't remembered him telling me he was coming over.

"I woke up thinking that I really wanted to go and get a cup of coffee with my girl. Figured if I just showed up, you couldn't tell me no."

I smiled. "You know I wouldn't have said no."

"Why is it so cold in here?" Justin asked as he sat down to wait for me to dress.

"If you would've called first then I would have been dressed and ready by the time you got here and you wouldn't have to freeze waiting on me."

"I wanted to surprise you," Justin said. He rubbed his hands together like he was trying to warm himself. "Holy shit, it's freaking cold in here. Don't tell me you like it like this?"

"No, I don't," I said emerging from my bedroom in a pair of jeans and a sweater. "But it's not like I have a choice on the temperature. The landlord decides what it gets set to."

"So you're telling me it's this cold in here all winter long?"

"No, sometimes it's colder," I said, grabbing my coat from the closet.

A few minutes later Justin and I made it to the coffee shop, where it was nice and warm inside. I'd almost forgotten how nice that felt. We found a small table in the corner and Justin reached for my still cold hand. "What can I do?"

"About what?"

"You can't stay in that freezing apartment all winter long."

"Yes, I can." Justin didn't seem convinced. "I do have a space heater you know. I just haven't pulled it out of my closet yet."

"Those things are dangerous, they catch fire all the time."

"Justin, can we change the subject, please? I've told you a million times, I'm a big girl, and I'll be fine."

"I can't help it, Jess. I worry about you; and you never let me help you."

"You help me all the time."

Justin gave me another skeptical look. He'd been offering to help me get another apartment for the past few weeks. I knew I should've felt grateful that he wanted to help, but instead I just felt humiliated. "Fine. I won't bring it up anymore. Anyway, the reason I just sort of showed up this morning is because I had something I wanted to ask you."

"What is it?"

"I was hoping you'd agree to come to my house for Thanksgiving this year."

"Your family will be there," I said, stating the obvious.

"Of course they will be. I thought you might finally want to meet them."

Secretly I'd wondered when Justin was ever going to introduce me to his family. We'd been dating almost three months and I'd never met a single friend or family member of his. Now that he'd extended the invitation I was petrified by the prospect.

"Your family?"

Justin nodded.

"Did you already tell them you were planning on asking your girlfriend to come over for Thanksgiving?" Justin had said that he told his family about me, but how much they really knew, I wasn't sure.

"I told them." Justin took a sip of coffee and then set his cup back down on the saucer.

"And what did they say?" I got the distinct impression that Justin was keeping some vital piece of information from me. I could always tell when he was anxious about something.

"Nothing, really. They all want to meet you. It's just that, I told you, my mom can be kind of protective. Especially after what happened with my ex."

"You don't think she'll like me?"

Justin fidgeted in his chair. He was doing a poor job at hiding the fact that he was uncomfortable about what he was about to say. "It's just that I think it's for the best if you didn't tell her that much about yourself. If you kept to the basics like what you're majoring in, how we met, that kind of thing. You can tell her you live in Brooklyn, but maybe don't mention the exact area. Park Slope is real nice. Just tell her you live close to Park Slope."

"So you want me to lie?"

"It's not really a lie."

"It takes me twenty minutes to get to Park Slope from my house, how is that considered close?"

"The less my mother knows, the better."

"That doesn't make any sense. You want me to meet your family so we can get to know each other, but then you don't want me telling them anything about myself." It's not like I was planning on pouring my entire life story out, but the way Justin was talking it made me wonder if he was ashamed of me. It was just one more thing to add to the pile, one more thing for me to worry and feel insecure about, and suddenly, it felt like I'd reached my tipping point.

"That's not exactly what…"

I reached inside my pocket for the few dollars I had and flung them on the table before Justin could explain himself. I stood up and stormed out of the coffee shop. Something had told me all along there was a reason why I hadn't met his family. I was good enough for a weekend of fun, and that was about it. Hot tears streamed down my face as I marched down the street and towards the subway station. I could hear Justin calling my name, but I ignored him and kept walking faster and faster. Halfway down the stairs of the closest station I felt Justin close his hand around my arm. I spun around to face him.

"Let go."

"Not until you tell me what the hell is going on with you."

"What is going on is that I want to be alone right now." I tried grabbing my arm away from Justin, but his grip was firm. A train must have just stopped and let off a load of passengers because suddenly it felt like we were swarmed as people trudged up the stairs knocking into us. I didn't want to make a scene in public.

"Fine," I said. "But not here." Justin followed me down into the train station. I slid my card through the card reader and handed it to Justin to do the same. I walked towards the front of the train platform hoping that there weren't many people around and stood there with my arms crossed in front of me.

"I'm waiting," Justin said.

"There's nothing to say. If you're ashamed of me then I don't have to meet your family, but I don't appreciate you asking me to lie to them, it's like you're telling me I'm not good enough."

"That's not what I was trying to say. It's just that I know how my mother is and I just want to protect you from her. Once she gets to know you and sees how wonderful and beautiful you are then it won't matter." Justin moved closer to me. I could tell he wanted to wrap his arms around me, but I turned my back to him so he wouldn't see the fresh tears that started rolling down my face. *Why was I so angry with him?* It occurred to me then what was eating at me. Weeks of worrying about things I had no control over were wearing on me. I was good at keeping my feelings bottled up until something set me off and then I blew up. Between worrying about the fact that I was holding my brother back from the life he deserved, stressing over the loneliness that Thanksgiving and Christmas brought, and the prospect of spending another freezing cold winter suffering through my landlord's refusal to supply heat I was close to the edge.

"I just think it's better if I go to Mel's for Thanksgiving." I wouldn't have to pretend at her house. There would be more food than I could eat in a week, there would be music and jokes and laughter and no pressure to act like someone I wasn't. So what if one of her cousins got drunk and tried grabbing my ass. It would still be a million times easier dealing with that than trying to impress Justin's uptight family.

"I'm going with you then."

I shook my head. It was still turned so Justin couldn't see my face. I didn't want to speak because I was afraid he'd hear the sadness in my voice.

"You're killing me here, Jess," Justin pleaded. "I'm sorry. I shouldn't have told you how to act. You know I think you're perfect just the way you are."

"You're wrong. I'm so far away from perfect." I was right. My voice had given me away. Justin came around from behind me before I had a chance to turn away again. He saw the salty trail that the tears that streaked down my face had left behind.

"Why are you crying?"

I wiped my eyes. "I'm not. I'm just cold. The wind makes my eyes tear."

"You don't really think I'm going to buy that." Justin waited for me to answer, but I didn't want to tell him what I was feeling. "Jess, please talk to me."

"I told you I wanted to be alone."

Justin reached out and held the sides of my face with his hands. "I'm not going anywhere until you tell me what's going on."

I buried my head in Justin's chest as fresh tears erupted from my eyes. "I hate Thanksgiving and I hate Christmas and I hate the winter because it's so damn cold and my brother's probably going to get married soon and then I'll *never* see him, not like I see him that much now, but still…"

I was bawling like a baby and sure that not much of it made sense to Justin. I wasn't even sure he could hear me since my head was still buried in his chest and my words were muffled by his coat.

Justin put his arms around me and started stroking the back

of my hair. "Why do you hate Christmas?"

"What is there for me to like about it? Everyone else I know spends the day with their family eating Christmas cookies and opening presents while I'm home alone or with some friend that invited me over because they felt sorry for me."

"You don't have to be alone ever again, Jess. I want you to spend Christmas with me."

"And with your mom who is probably going to hate my guts?"

"She'll love you, and even if she doesn't, I don't care. I love you and that's all that matters."

I mopped my eyes with one my sleeves. "I love you, too," I said. "And I'm sorry I got so mad."

"Why won't you let me help you find another apartment?" Justin offered again. "Someplace where you won't freeze to death."

"My apartment's cold, but it's not that cold. I'll be fine once I pull out the space heater." And I would be, but I still hated the reminder that I was stuck in a life I never imagined for myself. Sometimes it felt like the only good things in it were the hope of something better one day after I was done with school and Justin. But I hated hanging my happiness on another person, there was just too much that could go wrong. My own life, the path I took, was under my control, but I had no control when it came to Justin. He could turn his back on me whenever he wanted just like my parents had done, and then where would I be?

"Have I ever told you that I hate your apartment? I hate your neighborhood. If I helped you find another place it wouldn't just be for you, it would make me feel better, too."

"I can't afford anything better and I'm not going to let you pay my rent."

Justin groaned. "I knew you'd say that. I don't get why you won't let me help you."

"We've talked about that already." I shivered. Even wrapped in Justin's arms it was cold.

"Let's go somewhere. Somewhere warm. You barely touched your coffee and it's practically lunch time by now."

I wanted to protest, to tell Justin I was fine and that I wasn't hungry. Susan, who was Catholic, had explained to me at one point about the seven deadly sins, and I realized that mine was most definitely pride. But even my pride had its limits, and, at that moment, I was too cold to argue with Justin.

Chapter 15

Opening up to Justin helped. Once everything, or at least most of it, was off my chest I felt like I was able to breathe again and see things from a different perspective. Or maybe I was just too anxious about finally meeting Justin's family to think about much of anything else. Justin insisted that one way or another we were spending Thanksgiving together, and I figured I wouldn't be scoring any points with Justin's family if I stole him away from them at a major holiday.

Mike and Melanie kept asking me if I was sure I didn't want to spend Thanksgiving with them. I was tempted to say yes and bring Justin along with me. The night before Thanksgiving Mel stayed over. She and my brother spent half of it in the kitchen preparing food to bring back to her mom's house the next day.

The banging around of pots and pans woke me up way too early Thanksgiving morning.

"I thought you two were done already?" I said as I walked into the kitchen still half-asleep. "Who wakes up this early on a national holiday anyway?"

"Mel decided we needed to make another tray of macaroni and

cheese. Because three just aren't enough," my brother groaned.

"You know how big my family is," Mel said to my brother. I sat down at the table with a bowl and a box of cereal and Mel turned to ask me, "You sure you don't want to come over?"

"What, and miss your cousins hitting on her all night?" Mike said.

"I promised Justin I'd go to his house."

"You'll miss my famous mac and cheese."

"This is the first time you're meeting Justin's family, right?" Mike asked.

I nodded. Mel turned around. "Oh my God, on Thanksgiving, too? That is what I call pressure. Do you have any idea what they're like?"

"Not really. Justin doesn't talk that much about his family, except for his mom. He said she's sort of protective. She's the one I'm really worried about."

"Don't tell me he's a mama's boy. Those are the worst."

"I don't think he is."

"Then why is he still living at home? He really needs to get his own place."

"Mel," my brother warned. "It's none of our business."

"I'm just saying, a twenty-five year old man is not supposed to be living at his parent's house."

"It's because of his legs," I explained. "He's worried he can't handle things if he lived on his own."

"That's bullshit. There's plenty of amputees who live on their own. Is he planning on living with his family forever?"

"I don't know, we haven't really talked about it. He gets kind of funny when I bring up the subject, and I don't want to push.

I think there's more to it than Justin lets on."

"It's his PTSD," Mike said, matter-of-factly. He had a way of getting straight to the point of things.

"I don't want to talk about this anymore." I got up from the table. Out of the corner of my eye I saw Mel and Mike glancing at each other and knew they had plenty more they wanted to say. I wondered some of the same things Mel did, but I felt like Justin and I hadn't been together long enough for me to ask the questions I wanted answers to. I figured that with enough time, things would sort themselves out.

After a long hot shower, I got dressed. I chose a pair of black dress pants and topped it with a warm burgundy colored sweater. I wore my hair loose and put on a little eye shadow and lip-gloss.

"You look real pretty," Mel commented as I stepped out of my bedroom.

"Thanks." I put my coat on and turned towards my brother and his girlfriend. "Wish me luck."

"You don't need it, J. I have the most awesome sister on the planet, and if Justin and his family don't know it, Mel has a few cousins that can fight it out over you." Mel swatted my brother with the dishrag in her hands. "I'm just saying," Mike said.

Mel walked up to me and gave me a hug. "Happy Thanksgiving."

It was freezing outside even though the sun was shining brightly. Justin wanted to pick me up and bring me over to his place, but I insisted on riding the train on my own and eventually Justin backed off. I was bringing a traditional Croatian dessert with me that I'd baked the night before. Kiflice was a cookie that sort of looked like a small croissant and was stuffed with jam in the middle.

The trains were running slow because of the holiday and I wound up almost half an hour late to Justin's building. As I made my way up the elevator my stomach churned with nervous anxiety. The door to Justin's apartment was open and he stood at the entrance waiting for me. I kissed him on his cheek and he took the plate of cookies from my hands. I followed him inside and tried to act as normal as I knew how to as I took everything in. A large foyer led into a living room that was bigger than my entire apartment. Justin came back from wherever he'd disappeared with the plate of cookies. He held my hand as we walked towards the seating area. His parents sat beside each other on a plush dark brown leather loveseat. They stood as I approached.

"Mom. This is Jessica." Justin snaked his arm around my waist.

"We've heard so much about you," Justin's mom said with a smile painted on her face. She extended a bony hand for me to shake. Justin's mom was tall and slender and looked older than I'd pictured in my mind. Her ash blonde hair fell in face framing layers and was definitely the work of an expensive uptown hair salon.

"It's nice to meet you Mrs. and Mr. Lambert."

Justin's dad shook my hand next. "Would you like something to drink? I have some white chilling. There's also an excellent Merlot if you prefer red."

"No thanks. I'm fine."

I wondered where Justin's brothers were and was about to ask him when I heard two male voices. "Your brothers?"

Justin nodded as they entered the living room.

"James, Jeff," he called out to them. "This is Jessica."

"Holy shit, all these J names are going to drive me crazy," the taller one said as he walked over to me with his hand outstretched. "You're a lot prettier than I thought you'd be."

Mrs. Lambert swatted her son's arm. She had a shocked look on her face. "Jeff!"

"He's always had a problem keeping his mouth shut," Justin whispered in my ear.

"It's all right." I smiled.

"How about I show you around?" Justin suggested.

He led me through the living room towards the dining area. A large table was set with gorgeous crisp linens in earth tones. The kitchen was just off the dining area and was also huge. I felt like I was in a home straight out of HGTV. Justin showed me where a bathroom was next, then he pointed to a few bedrooms before opening the door to his. In the corner of his room I spotted his wheelchair and a few canes and braces that he must have used when he was learning to get around on his prosthetics. When we got back to the living room, Justin's parents were setting food out on the table.

"Do you need any help with anything?" I asked.

"We're just about finished," Justin's mother replied curtly.

I sat down beside Justin on one of the couches and tried my best not to stare. Even when I was younger and still lived with my parents I'd never stepped foot in a place as nice as Justin's home. Besides the fact that it was huge, it was so clean and bright. Huge, practically floor to ceiling windows let in tons of natural light. The apartment was decorated in shades of tan and brown. Paintings on the wall and vases on side tables added splashes of just the right amount of bright color to the neutral palette. The floors were hardwood covered with expensive area rugs, the furniture leather. Photos of Justin and his brothers were hung on one of the walls. There were pictures of them as babies, school, and graduation photos. But no pictures of Justin in his Navy uniform, something I'd really wanted to see. I couldn't think of an apartment more different from my own than this. Justin must have been in shock the first time he saw my place.

A few minutes later Justin's parents were finished and called us to the table. Mr. Lambert carved the turkey and a platter was passed around the table. Besides turkey, the Lamberts served stuffing, salad and sweet potatoes. Everything was so fancy, too fancy. It made me miss the way things were at Mel's family's house where no one would notice or care if I didn't use the right kind of fork.

"This turkey is delicious," I said, hoping Justin's mom would appreciate the compliment. It really was good, not dry like turkey usually was.

Jeff snickered and I cast a sideways glance at Justin hoping he might clue me in as to what was so funny.

"My mom doesn't cook. She got all the food from a caterer," Justin explained. "She's not exactly what you would call a chef."

"Not exactly a chef?" Jeff laughed. "If by that you mean she never cooks, then yeah, she's not exactly a chef."

"Oh, I'm sorry, I didn't know."

"Of course you didn't," Mrs. Lambert said. I had no idea what she meant by that, but it felt like she was insulting me.

"So," Mrs. Lambert began. "How long have you and my son been friends?"

"Mom. I told you already," Justin chimed in. "She's my girlfriend."

"Uch." Mrs. Lambert waved her hand. "Friend, girlfriend, what's the difference?"

"Actually mom, there's a pretty big difference," Jeff interjected.

Mrs. Lambert was still looking at me as if she was awaiting my response. "We met in June. I was working at the community center over the summer."

"But not anymore?"

"No." I shook my head.

"So what do you do?"

"I'm in college. Junior year, education major."

"So you plan on being a teacher?"

"Yup, that's the plan."

"I detect an accent. Where are you from?"

It was total BS. I knew I didn't have an accent. "I'm Croatian," I told her. "But I was actually born here."

"Hmm. Is that right?" Justin's mom took a sip of her wine. "Has Justin met your family yet?"

"Just my brother."

"Well maybe we can have them over sometime."

"That sounds nice," I said even though I knew it would never happen. But I had no intention of talking about my family situation with Justin's mother. "Do you mind if I use the bathroom?" I got up from the table and went in search of the bathroom Justin had shown me earlier. I needed a moment away from Justin's mother. Her thinly veiled hostility was putting me on edge.

After taking a few deep breaths and washing my face with

some cold water I returned to the dining room. Thankfully Mrs. Lambert did not resume her barrage of questions. Jeff and his dad were deep in a discussion about what he was going to do after he graduated while James was busy talking to Justin and his mother about the classes he was taking.

We finished eating and while everyone else made their way back to the living room Jeff began to clear the table.

"Let me help you," I said.

"That'd be great."

I followed his lead and stacked the plates near the sink. "I can start washing these dishes if you want," I offered.

Jeff started to laugh, and I felt awkward because I didn't know why. "You were serious?" he said, when he noticed I wasn't laughing along with him. "We have someone who'll come by later and take care of that."

"Oh. Right." I wasn't sure what else to say

Jeff grabbed two pies from the refrigerator and set them down on the gigantic kitchen island beside the cookies I'd brought. "So what do you think of my mother?"

"She's…uh. She seems nice."

Jeff laughed again. "You're a terrible liar. I don't think anyone's ever used that word to describe her."

"I don't think she likes me very much."

"Don't take it personal. I doubt my mom would like any girl Justin brought home."

"Why? You'd think after everything Justin went through that she'd want him to be happy."

"She doesn't believe that Justin can live a normal life again, and I think she's okay with that. She sees him as her little pet that she plans on keeping by her side for the rest of her life. She never wanted him to join the Navy to begin with, so when he almost died it really hit her hard."

"That's not fair to Justin."

"Yeah, I know," he conceded. "I actually feel really bad for what happened to him and not just for the obvious reasons. This life isn't the one he wanted. You should have seen him when he finished boot camp. He was so proud, so happy to be doing something different with his life than the rest of us. And now look at him. If it were up to Justin he'd be outside playing football with a bunch of guys instead of in here watching it on TV." Jeff took the foil off the plate of cookies I'd brought and popped one in his mouth. "Mmmm, these are so good. Did you make them?"

"Yeah," I replied blankly, still processing what Jeff had just told me.

"That's awesome. We get to have something homemade for Thanksgiving this year after all."

"Can I ask you something?"

"Sure."

"How come there's no pictures of Justin in his uniform in your house?"

"He doesn't like to be reminded of being in the Navy. When he joined I think he was sure he'd be in for life and then…well you know what happened. Losing your legs kind of ruins a military career, and Justin's still pretty bitter about it."

Jeff turned and started walking towards the dining room.

"Jeff." He turned his head. "Why did you just tell me what you did about Justin and your mom?"

"You seem real nice, and you've made Justin happier than I've seen him since he was sent to Afghanistan. I just thought you deserved to know what you were up against. For what it's worth, I hope you win."

Great, just great. I wasn't even sure what he meant when he said that he hoped I'd win, but I was certain it wasn't good.

Chapter 16

Jeff finished brewing a pot of coffee and we all returned to the table for dessert. Except I wasn't in the mood for it. Jeff's words of warning made me more tense and anxious than I already had been. Having your boyfriend's mother hate you was hard enough under normal circumstances, but with Justin it seemed like an impossible obstacle. Which meant I had no choice but to find a way to make her like me. Problem was, I had no idea how to do that.

Later, when we were all back in the living room and the men were focused on the football game they were watching I tried to think of something to say to strike up a conversation with Mrs. Lambert.

"Your house is really beautiful," I finally said.

"Thank you."

"Have you lived here for a long time?"

"A little over ten years, I think. Justin's father and I were thinking about putting it on the market and getting a smaller place, but then Justin came back home and I was glad we held on to it. This is Justin's home. After everything he went through it's what he needed."

"Justin's lucky to have you guys."

Mrs. Lambert gave me another one of her forced smiles. "And now he has you, too." Mrs. Lambert had a knack for saying things that I wasn't really sure how to interpret. The football game was winding down, and no matter how comfortable and nice Justin's apartment was, I felt ready to go back home because I wasn't sure how much longer I could keep myself from saying something stupid or embarrassing.

After the TV was turned off, I stood. "I should get going." Everyone turned to look at me. "Thank you for inviting me over. It was nice meeting all of you."

"I'm going with you," Justin said.

"You don't have to do that. I'm fine."

"It's dark out."

Justin got up, followed by his brother who clapped him on the back. "You did good, Justin," Jeff said.

"Would you stop ogling your brother's friend already," Mrs. Lambert said. There was that friend word again. It was like she steadfastly refused to believe her son and I had anything romantic going on.

"I'm not ogling her." He turned to look at his brother, but didn't wait for a reply. "You know I'm not, right? I'm just saying she's pretty, and she's nice, and she bakes some damn good cookies."

"Language, mister," Justin's mother said.

"I should get going," I said again.

"Oh, wait." Mrs. Lambert walked over to the table and came back with the half-eaten plate of cookies I'd brought. "Don't forget your cookies."

"They were supposed to be for you."

"And they were lovely." Another fake smile. "But we're trying to watch how much sugar we eat."

I took the cookies from her and followed Justin into the foyer where my coat was hanging. He helped me into it and the two of us left together.

"Holy crap. I do not think your mother likes me one bit," I said when we got outside.

"She doesn't like anyone at first." Justin reached for my hand. "Once she gets to know you she'll warm up, I promise."

I didn't want to bring up what Jeff had said. I figured Justin wouldn't enjoy being referred to as someone's pet, and I wanted to believe that Justin's opinion of the situation was the right one, not Jeff's.

"You know you really don't have to walk me to the train station. I'll be fine. It's Thanksgiving, you should be with your family."

"It's dark out. I'm not letting you go home alone."

"You know I hate it when you tell me you're not going to let me do something."

"C'mon. You know I didn't mean it like that." Justin stopped walking, I turned to see why. "I don't want to say goodnight yet."

"It's freezing out here, Justin. And we ate a big meal for lunch, so I'm not hungry and I'm not in the mood for a movie." The truth was I just wanted to go home. Justin's house was beautiful and warm, but I felt so uncomfortable there. All I wanted to do was take a hot shower and crawl under *my* covers in *my* apartment where I didn't have to worry about doing or saying the wrong thing.

Justin reached for my hand, the one stuffed into my pocket so it wouldn't turn into an icicle like the one that was holding the cookies Justin's mom had given back to me. She hadn't even tried one. I felt like an idiot for bothering.

"I want to spend the night with you again."

"Justin, I don't know." His suggestion took me by surprise. "I don't have a change of clothes or a toothbrush or anything."

"Then we'll get some things from your apartment first." He had a pleading look on his face that made it impossible to say no. "Please." Justin took a step closer and brushed his lips on mine. "I miss holding you and touching you."

"What about your stuff?"

"I don't need anything, just you."

I pressed my lips to Justin's. "Okay." I did not know how to say no to him.

We got in a cab that drove us to my apartment. The driver waited while I ran inside to fill an overnight bag with a few things. Justin had him take us back to the same hotel where we'd spent my birthday weekend. In the room, Justin opened a bottle of champagne and poured glasses for both of us. Before I had a chance to finish mine, Justin's lips found mine. He kissed me hungrily and reached under my shirt. His hands cupped my breasts. He pulled my shirt off, then his. The two of us tumbled onto the bed kissing and undressing each other at the same time.

"Oh God, I missed you so much." I shivered as Justin's tongue brushed my nipple. My fingers raked down his back as I pressed my body against his. Justin panted and moaned as he slid into me. Every cell in my body burned with desire until I was totally and completely consumed.

"I wish we could do that every night," Justin said as we lay beside each other later.

"Who knows?" I grinned, still feeling blissful. "Maybe someday we can."

Justin didn't say anything, instead he reached for another glass of champagne.

"Can I ask you something?"

"What is it?"

"Did your mother like your ex?"

Justin furrowed his brow. "Where did that come from?"

"I'm just curious."

"She liked her. But the circumstances were different. I knew her since we were kids, our parents were friendly with each other, and we went to the same school…"

"Right, right. I get it."

Justin turned on his side to face me. "Can we not talk about my mom or my ex anymore? Please. Those are the last two people I want to think about when I'm with you."

"Fine." I got out of bed and headed towards the bathroom. Not because I really had to go, but because I was starting to get upset and didn't want Justin to see it.

"Is something wrong?" Justin asked.

"No." I shook my head trying to convince myself that it didn't matter that Justin's mom had liked his ex, but that she clearly didn't like me. She was out of his life and Justin was with me and we loved each other and that would be enough to make everything right. Still, I couldn't help the doubts that were forming in my mind. "I'll be right back."

When I got my head together I went to lie back down next

to Justin who was drinking another glass of champagne. I nestled into his arms enjoying the warmth that radiated from his body. He stroked my hair tenderly as I lay beside him.

"Your hair is so soft, it feels like silk," Justin whispered. I looked up at him, his eyes locked on mine. "I love you so much, Jess,"

I reached out to touch his cheek. "I love you, too."

We talked for a while and, at some point, I remember Justin turning the TV on. My eyelids began to feel heavy and eventually I drifted off to sleep. I awoke sometime later to the sound of Justin screaming. The TV was still on so it was light enough in the room for me to see him thrashing around in bed.

"Justin. Justin." I shook him to try and wake him up and all of a sudden he pounced on me pinning me down flat on the bed. "Justin." I tried prying him off me, but it felt like he was a thousand pounds.

"Get off," I yelled and then pushed hard until Justin fell to my side. I turned on the bedside lamp. Justin sat up and looked around the room like he was in a daze.

"What the hell just happened?" I asked, rubbing my arms where Justin had grabbed them.

"A dream," Justin whispered. His eyes looked glazed, hollow. "I'm sorry. Did I hurt you?"

"No. You just scared me. Are you okay?"

"I didn't want that to happen around you," he mumbled so softly I barely heard him.

"Do you get dreams like that a lot?"

"No." He shook his head. "I usually take medication before I go to sleep, but it's at home. It keeps me from having dreams.

But I didn't really think about that when I asked you to spend the night with me."

I crept closer to Justin and wrapped my arms around the middle of his back. "Is it PTSD?"

Justin rested his head on my shoulder. "It's too much, isn't it?" he asked.

"What's too much?"

"Having no legs is bad enough. I can't ask you to deal with more than that."

"What are you saying, Justin?"

"That if you want to bail on me I get it. Who in their right mind would want to be with a double amputee with PTSD *and* have to deal with a mother like mine?"

"I don't want to bail on you, Justin. I love you."

"It'll be easier if you walk away now, before I fall even more in love with you than I already am," Justin whispered, his voice hoarse.

"Please don't say that to me again or I'm going to feel like it's what you want."

"You seemed so unhappy earlier after we left my apartment. I thought if we came back here I could make you forget what an awful time you had at my house."

"Is that why you were overdoing it on the champagne?"

"You noticed?"

I nodded. "It's not like you to drink that much."

"God, I'm so sorry. I was just upset about the way my mom treated you. I kept thinking that you wished you had gone with your brother instead."

"It wasn't that bad," I said. "Let's just forget about it, okay?

Justin nodded. I lay back down and pulled him down beside me. It was half past three and I was tired. "If I turn off the lights and we try and get some sleep, do you think you'll be okay?"

"Do you still love me, Jess?"

"Of course I do," I insisted, surprised that he could think otherwise.

Justin wrapped one of his arms over my shoulder. "Then I'll be all right."

I fell asleep faster than I expected to. In the morning when I woke up Justin was already dressed.

"Hey beautiful," he said.

"Is everything all right?"

"Yeah. Everything's fine." Justin came to sit beside me on the bed. He brushed my hair back with his hand. "Did you sleep all right?"

"Mmmm, I did."

"I want to spend the day with you, but I didn't bring a change of clothes with me. I really should get back home and shower and change."

"Don't worry about it. I have a ton of laundry to do and school work to catch up on."

"Can I see you tomorrow?"

We always spent Saturdays together. "Of course."

Chapter 17

The last few weeks of the semester flew by in a blur of final papers and exams. When I handed in my last exam I breathed a sigh of relief. I finally had enough free time that I could hang out with Susan again, squeeze in some Christmas shopping, and still have time with Justin. But the closer to Christmas it got, the more nervous I became. First off, I had no idea what to buy Justin, I couldn't afford to buy him the same type of presents he got me, but I wanted to get him something he'd really love. But the thing that made me the most anxious was the thought of the Christmas Eve dinner that Justin had invited me to at his house.

"I promise my mother will be nicer this time," Justin said after asking me to come.

I wasn't convinced. "I'm not going to be able to afford to buy presents for everyone in your family." I was trying to come up with a reason why I wouldn't be able to go.

"You don't need to buy any presents, Jess," Justin said. "C'mon, this is going to be our first Christmas together and I want to spend it with you."

I agreed only because I wanted to spend Christmas with

Justin. His family, not so much, but they were a part of his life.

Mike had been putting in a crazy amount of overtime so he could pay for Melanie's engagement ring so it didn't surprise me that by the time I was ready to go to Justin's I hadn't seen him. I sent him a text on my way to the train station.

Merry Christmas Mike. Tell Mel I said hi.

Merry Christmas to you too J wish me luck.

He wouldn't need it. Mel would say yes. And with that happy thought in my head I ran down the stairs of the Carroll Street station headed for Justin's with his present tucked under my arm.

A little over an hour later the doorman announced my arrival. Justin's apartment had looked nice on Thanksgiving, but between the gigantic Christmas tree in the living room and the decorations adorning the rest of the living space, it looked magical this time.

"My mother tends to go all out for Christmas," Justin explained as he noticed me staring.

The mantle by the fireplace held four red velvet stockings and was covered with sprigs of holly and twinkling white Christmas lights. Every doorway was decorated with red ribbon twisted around evergreen garlands. The apartment smelled gloriously of pine.

Justin's dad and brothers greeted me warmly with hugs and wishes for a Merry Christmas, while his mother eyed me suspiciously. She barely spoke to me during dinner. It wasn't until after we ate, while Justin's family was tearing open presents sent from various family and friends that Justin's mother sat beside me.

"I was surprised when Justin said you were coming to have

Christmas Eve dinner with us."

"Why's that?"

She looked at me like she didn't believe I didn't already know what was on her mind. I didn't, but I had a feeling it wasn't going to good. "I love my son dearly," she finally said. "But he isn't exactly what most young girls are looking for."

I kept myself from saying what I really wanted to. "What is it that you think most girls are looking for?"

"I'm sure you're aware of Justin's issues."

"I am, and I love him just the way he is."

The look of doubt still hadn't left Mrs. Lambert's face despite my assertion. "Hmm. So what did my son get you for Christmas?"

"I don't know. We decided to exchange our presents later, privately."

"No doubt he got you something extravagant. Like the necklace you're wearing now."

My fingers brushed over the present Justin had given me at the end of summer. How did she know it was a gift from him? "Excuse me," I said. I was getting more uncomfortable by the minute. "I need to go use the bathroom."

The moment I locked the bathroom door behind me I let out a sigh. After Thanksgiving I was pretty sure Justin's mother didn't like me, now there was no doubt. The only thing I didn't know was what in the world I was going to do about it.

I tried to keep a safe distance between Mrs. Lambert and myself after returning from the bathroom. Every time I glanced in her direction I would've sworn she was looking at me out of the corner of her eyes like she was making sure I wasn't secretly pocketing her silverware.

"I need to get some fresh air," Jeff announced after most of the presents were opened and the wrapping paper was cleared off the floor. "Who wants to come with?"

"You want to go?" I asked Justin, eager to get out of his house and away from his mother.

"It's okay. You go ahead. I need to talk to my mother about something."

The cold air filled my lungs as I stepped outside with Jeff. No one else had wanted to join us and I realized why. The air felt like a knife. "You don't like cold, do you?" Jeff asked as we headed up the street.

"No." I shivered as a strong wind seemed to push cold air through my coat. "I actually hate it, but I needed…"

"To get away from my mother."

I smiled, but didn't reply. Jeff already knew without needing me to confirm it.

"Well, if it's worth anything I'm glad she hasn't chased you off. I was worried she might've after Thanksgiving."

"So was Justin." I thought carefully about what to say next. "He was upset that night. I had to wake him up from some crazy dream he was having. He was worried that between his legs and his PTSD and your mother, who obviously hates me that I'd bail on him."

"But you didn't."

"I love him." I paused trying to collect my thoughts. "You know the funny thing is his legs and PTSD don't really bother me. I mean I feel bad about what he went through and all, but the way your mother treats me is harder to deal with than anything else."

"I'll talk to her."

It was a nice offer, but I wasn't sure it would make much of a difference. "You know what? I really am freezing. Do you mind if I head back without you?"

"No, go ahead. I'll see you at the house later."

I practically ran back to Justin's building eager to escape the cold. The doorman remembered me from earlier and just waved as I walked past him and onto the elevator. As I approached the door to Justin's apartment, I heard voices. Justin's and his mother's. The closer I got to the door the clearer they became.

"You need to lay off, Mom. I'm not kidding."

"I'm just trying to protect you."

"I don't need you to protect me, and even if I did, I don't need to be protected from Jessica. She's my girlfriend, we love each other."

"You mean you love her, and she loves your money."

I sucked in my breath, shocked that Justin's mother would say that about me. She barely knew me. There was a moment of silence after that. A part of me felt like running, another part of me felt like I needed to hear the rest of their conversation.

"I'm going to pretend you did not just say that." The anger in Justin's voice was impossible to miss, even through the closed door.

"What do you even know about that girl? For all you know she could be planning on sending our money back to her family in whatever country she's from."

"What I know is that she'll be back any second now and I don't want her hearing any more bullshit from you."

How was I going to face Justin's mother after those words?

Sure, she hadn't said them to me, but I'd heard them, and there was no taking that back.

I ran back towards the elevator and when it opened I got on and rode it back downstairs, then all the way back to Justin's floor. I did that two more times and even though I was still hurt and angry I knew I had to go back to Justin's. If Jeff came back without me, Justin would demand to know where I'd been, and I wasn't ready to talk about what I'd heard his mother say.

I had no idea how things between me and Justin were ever going to work out when his mother hated me as much as she did. I knew she wasn't my biggest fan, but I never thought she took me for a gold digger. It was so crazy, too, because Justin was always insisting on taking me to fancy places and buying me beautiful presents, and I was always telling him it was too much. If anything I wished Justin had less money, so I didn't always feel so inadequate around him.

I knocked on the door to Justin's apartment. He opened it with a smile, not a trace of the anger I'd heard in his voice earlier remained. It was as if the conversation he'd had with his mother hadn't taken place, except that it had.

"I made you some hot chocolate," Justin said as he helped me out of my coat. He craned his neck as if he were looking for something. "Where's Jeff?"

"Jeff?" I asked before I remembered that the two of us were supposed to be walking together. "I was getting cold so I came back without him. I'm sure he'll be back soon."

We made our way to the living room. I took the mug Justin handed to me, but couldn't bring myself to take even a sip. I felt sick to my stomach. Mrs. Lambert's insults rang in my ears. The last time someone's words had stung me so much was when they'd come from my father, and he was the last person I liked to be reminded of.

A few minutes passed, though it felt like hours. "You know what?" I said, standing up from the couch. "It's getting late."

"Already?" Justin asked.

"Yeah well, I'm kind of tired."

"Let me bring you home."

"No need. I can take the train. It'll be hard to find a taxi on Christmas Eve." Justin followed me to the doorway. He grabbed my arm as I reached for my coat.

"What's going on? "

"I'm just not feeling that well."

"I'm going with you then."

"No!" I said it a little too loudly. I lowered my voice to just above a whisper. "Your mother is going to hate me even more than she already does. I'll text you when I get home."

"Is everything all right?" Justin's mother strolled into the foyer.

"Yes, everything's fine. I'm going to bring Jess home and then I'll be back."

"It's not a good night to be out Justin. You know people like to get drunk on the holidays."

"I told him I can get home on my own just fine." I was still trying to extend an olive branch even after what I heard her say earlier.

"Well, I suppose you do have an incentive to make sure he's all right." Her tone was acerbic and again I was left to wonder exactly what she meant by her words.

"I'll see you later." I kissed Justin on his cheek and headed for the elevator. He stood in the doorway staring at me like he wasn't sure what to do. I waved as the elevator arrived and opened its doors.

When I made it to the lobby I practically ran outside of Justin's building. Despite how fast I was walking I barely made it halfway down the block when I heard Justin calling my name. I didn't feel like talking, but I didn't want to make him run after me, so I stopped and turned and waited for him.

"You should be with your family," I said after he caught up to me.

"I want to be with you."

"Please, Justin. Just go back home." I felt tears bubbling inside me and wanted to get as far away from Justin as I could before I let them out.

Justin reached into his coat and pulled out a small box and handed it to me. "You forgot your present."

"I don't need any more presents from you, you've already given me too much."

"For God's sake, Jess, it's Christmas. Take the present."

I reached for it and held it in my hand. Justin and I were supposed to be exchanging presents privately later so my sudden announcement that I was going home had probably come as a big surprise.

"Thank you." I tucked the present into my coat pocket. "It's cold out here, you should get back inside." I turned around, but as I walked away I could feel Justin's eyes on me. He didn't try to stop me, but I knew him well enough to realize that he was probably worried and upset so I texted him just before I got back home to let him know I was all right.

My apartment was freezing and painfully quiet. I turned my space heater up to high, took a hot shower and crawled into bed feeling numb. I never had been very good at letting things people said about me roll off my back. Mike and some of my friends told me I was too sensitive, and I knew they were right, but I couldn't help it. After the life I'd had, I should have built a tougher shell, but I hadn't.

In the morning I still felt awful. Justin had already called and left a message. I stared at the box he'd given me the night before, it lay unopened on my dresser. Finally, I picked up my phone to call him.

"Can I come see you?" Justin asked.

"Did you open your present?" I'd left it in his apartment.

"Not yet. I was still sort of hoping we could open our presents together."

"I'd like that. Mine's still unopened, too." I still hated spending time in my apartment with Justin, but it was Christmas and even in New York most places were closed, and it was too cold to be outside. I wasn't about to go back to his house, so that left only one option. "You can come over, if you like."

"I'll be there in twenty minutes."

Which meant I needed to get myself out of bed and into the shower and then find something to wear. "My place is a mess," I said as I opened the door and let him in less than an hour later. It was always a mess, even after I cleaned, but there wasn't much I could do about that.

"You know I don't care."

"I bet your mother would care. She'd probably have a heart attack if she saw my apartment."

"She'd have a heart attack if she saw a lot of things, but I'm not my mother." Justin had brought coffee and croissants with him. He took a bite of his breakfast and looked at me. "Is that why you practically ran out of my apartment yesterday? Did my mother say something to you?"

"She hates me." I bit the inside of my cheek and tried not to think about the hateful words I'd overheard her say.

"The way she acts has nothing to do with you, Jess. She thinks she's protecting me."

"It must be nice," I said, hearing the bitter in my voice. "Of course I wouldn't really know since I've never had anyone care enough to want to protect me."

"I care." When I didn't respond Justin reached for my hand. "You believe that, don't you?"

"You're my boyfriend, it's different."

"I'm not enough?"

Of course Justin didn't get it, why would he? He might have gone through a lot in Afghanistan and after he got home, but it was different than what I'd struggled with my whole life. His scars you could see, mine weren't visible, but they were still there.

"It's not that you're not enough, it's just that…well I already told you, Christmas is hard."

"But you're not alone anymore. We're together now, and last night…"

"Last night was a disaster, Justin. It was Christmas Eve and your mother made me feel like she didn't even want me in her home."

"Because she doesn't know the real you. Once she does things will be different."

"No. I don't think so. In fact I'm pretty sure if she knew the real me, she'd lock you in your bedroom and never let you come out."

"That's not true."

There was no point in arguing with Justin. He didn't want to see the truth, and I wasn't going to be able to make him. It was Christmas and the last thing I felt like doing was getting into an argument with Justin about his mother so I buried what I was feeling.

Justin had brought the present I'd left at his house with him. It rested on the table. I pushed the box towards him. "I want you to open your present first."

He reached for it hesitantly, held it to his ear and shook it.

I laughed. "Just open it."

Justin smiled and tore the wrapping paper off. As I watched him I couldn't help but think that even in the way we opened presents we were different. I never tore wrapping paper off gifts, I always opened them carefully so I could save the paper for another time. When you had as much money as Justin did, that was probably not even a consideration.

"Do you like it?" I asked as Justin took the top off the box and reached inside for the long sleeved tee and fleece workout pants I'd bought. "I know it's not much, but you look real nice in blue, and I thought for work these would be perfect."

"They are perfect, and I love them." Justin leaned towards me and kissed me.

"You're sure? Because I still have the receipt and you can exchange them for something you like better if you want."

"No. I'm not exchanging them, I love them," Justin said.

"Now it's your turn to open your present."

I headed to my bedroom to retrieve the box Justin had given me the night before and then rejoined him in the kitchen.

"Open it."

Inside the box was a platinum linked watch. I held it in my hands, my mouth open in awe as I took notice of the designer's name etched onto the face of the watch.

"It's so…nice." My description was woefully inadequate. "You shouldn't…"

"Don't tell me I shouldn't have. Just tell me you love it, that's all I want to hear."

"I love it." I leaped into his arms. It wasn't even the gift, it was knowing that Justin cared so much about making me happy that meant the most.

"I actually have one more thing for you." Justin eased me off his lap and got up to pull another box out of the inside pocket of his coat. He handed it to me, it was unwrapped so I knew right away what it was. "Justin! This is too much," I said as I stared at the box. He knew I loved to read and he'd bought me a mini tablet. I'd wanted one for a long time, but it wasn't something I would have ever been able to afford.

"You can bring it with you everywhere, because it's got a data plan."

"Oh my God, Justin. I can't believe this." I hugged him again.

"Just tell me you're happy, Jess."

I held Justin's chin in one hand and then kissed him hard and deep. "I'm happy."

"I felt so bad after you went home last night, because I knew you were upset, and I didn't know what to do."

"I wasn't mad at you."

"I knew why you were mad. After I got home, I talked to my mother again. So did my dad and my brothers."

"I don't want to talk about that anymore." I kissed Justin again and again.

"Oh, Jess. You don't know what you're doing to me."

"Actually, I do."

Mike had proposed to Mel or at least he was about to. If there was ever a time I was sure he wasn't going to walk in on me and Justin it was now. Justin kissed me back. He grabbed my hair with his hands and pressed me closer to him until I felt myself melt the way I always did when Justin had his hands on me. Somehow the two of us wound our way onto my bed. I climbed on top of Justin and made love to him until his body shook with pleasure.

We spent the rest of the day in bed and by the time Justin left later that evening my Christmas had turned out to be the best I'd ever remembered having.

Chapter 18

I didn't see my brother again until a few days after New Year. He came home one afternoon while I was busy sweeping the kitchen. He walked inside and I stood there staring at him, waiting for him to say something while he filled the freezer with a few quarts of his favorite Ben and Jerry's flavors.

"What?" he said after noticing me staring.

"Don't what me." I put my hands on my hips. "I want to know what Mel said, and don't leave anything out."

"She says a lot of things," Mike replied. He was smiling so I knew he was toying with me. I swatted him with the broom. "Hey, careful with that broom. You sweep that over my feet and I'll never get married."

"I didn't sweep it over your feet. And stop changing the subject," I said. "I want to know everything."

"Everything?" My brother cocked an eyebrow at me.

"No." I groaned. "I don't want to know about that. But I want to know everything else."

"Okay, okay." My brother sat down and I took the empty chair next to him.

"On Christmas Eve I took Mel out to dinner, somewhere really nice. You know how she likes Italian, right?"

I nodded.

"Anyway, I asked her while we were eating dessert. Tiramisu. And I'm pretty sure she had no idea. She acted really surprised."

"Did she like the ring?"

"She loved it. And she said yes."

"Of course she did." Mike had shown me the ring about two weeks before Christmas. It was perfect. My brother, who seemed to have friends everywhere, knew someone who worked in the Diamond District. He got a good deal on an emerald cut stone and then just took it somewhere to be set. It looked as nice as anything I'd ever seen in the windows at Tiffany, but he'd paid a lot less than what they charged. I hugged Mike. "I'm so happy for you."

"Thanks, J." Mike got up from the table after I released him from my embrace. "I feel like I can finally breathe again."

"You didn't really think she'd say no, did you?"

"I was a little worried," Mike admitted.

"Have you guys set a date yet?" I asked, trying to hide the worry from my voice. Once Mike and Mel were married I was out a roommate and trying to find another would be hard. I couldn't afford the rent on my own so I didn't have many options.

"Not yet. I know you can't pay for a place on your own yet, and you'll be done with school in a year and a half. I think we'll wait until then," my brother replied, as if he'd just read my mind.

"I don't want you to put your life on hold for me."

"A year and a half isn't that long. Mel and I can wait. Unless you think you might be able to move out sooner."

"I don't see that happening."

"What about you and Justin?"

"We've been going out for four months, it's a little too soon to be thinking about moving in together."

"He can't live with his parents forever, and the two of you are pretty serious aren't you?"

I nodded. "Yeah."

"It's the ideal situation then. He's afraid to be on his own, but now he has you. You can't afford an apartment by yourself, so now you have him."

"It's not that simple, Mike." Besides I hardly wanted to move in with someone because neither of us had any other good options.

"What's the problem?"

"Besides the fact that Justin's mom hates me? She'd probably put a hit out on me if Justin told her we were moving in together."

Mike looked at me like I was exaggerating until I told him what I'd overheard Mrs. Lambert say to Justin about me on Christmas Eve. His eyes grew wide and he exclaimed, "That bitch!"

"What am I supposed to do?"

"I don't know. But that's some fucked up shit right there." *Just great,* I thought. If Mike had no advice to offer, I was basically screwed. He always seemed to know how to figure out a way around things. "And you're telling me Justin doesn't know you heard what his mother said about you?"

"No. I didn't see any point in bringing it up. The situation is what it is."

~

Justin and I never discussed his mother anymore. Whenever I thought about the way she felt about me, it was like a cloud hanging over my head, and I chose to ignore it in the hopes that somehow the problem would magically vanish.

But Justin's birthday was approaching. In March he'd turn twenty-six, and we'd already planned to spend his birthday weekend together, until Justin's mother decided she wanted to throw a party for him.

"I don't think I should go," I said after Justin told me about it. "We can just meet afterwards."

"You're my girlfriend, Jess. You can't not come."

"I'm pretty sure your mother would prefer if I didn't." Even though we hadn't talked about her since Christmas, I knew a conversation about her was inevitable.

"Are you just never going to come to my apartment again?" Justin asked.

I nodded. "Pretty much, yeah."

Justin sighed. "I know she hasn't been the friendliest, but she'll never come around if you hide from her."

"I'm not hiding. And I really don't think it's fair for you to basically ask me to kiss her ass until she decides I'm good enough for you."

"That's not what I'm doing."

"I don't want to talk about this anymore. I'm not going, and that's final. If you don't want to spend the weekend with me, that's fine." I hated that Justin didn't even try to see my point of view.

"C'mon, Jess. Don't be like that."

I felt embarrassed about my little outburst, especially because we were in a public place and there were people around that could possibly overhear the two of us arguing. It was an unseasonably warm March day and after months of cold, gray weather I was grateful for some warmth and sunshine so the two of us were enjoying a spring picnic in the park.

For a moment I was tempted to explain myself to Justin, but I changed my mind. He wouldn't get it, he'd never understand things from my point of view.

Justin reached for my hand and laced his fingers through mine. "The truth is, I'm not in the mood for a party. I hate the attention and I'd much rather spend time with you alone."

"You shouldn't miss it because of me."

"The only reason why I agreed to the stupid party in the first place was to make my mom happy. After everything she's done for me, I don't like letting her down."

"You don't owe her for taking care of you, that's what mothers are supposed to do." It was funny hearing those words come out of my mouth. I had a mother, but even though she was supposed to have taken care of me, she hadn't. I sighed and slumped my shoulders as I realized how wrong what I'd just said was. "If it makes you happy, I'll go to your party."

"No." Justin shook his head. "I don't want a party. I don't want to be stuck inside with a bunch of people asking me to tell them war stories, and that's always how it is when my mother throws one of her get-togethers. I'll just tell her we already had plans."

"You sure?"

Justin nodded. "I'm sure."

On the Friday before his birthday, Justin left work early to pick me up. After we checked into our hotel room the two of us walked across the street to Central Park. The weather was still gorgeous, sunny and warm with just a slight breeze that made the branches of the trees sway. As the sun began to set, the wind picked up speed and I regretted leaving my jacket behind as it started to get chilly. A strong breeze left me with goose bumps on my arms.

"C'mon," Justin said noticing that I was getting cold. "Let's get something to eat."

We walked a little farther until we reached Tavern on the Green. The restaurant was packed inside and out, which would have normally meant a long wait, but we were led right away to an empty table.

"I made reservations," Justin explained as the two of us were seated.

I sighed. "You weren't supposed to do that. It's your birthday…"

"Exactly. And what I want for my birthday is another weekend with you."

Justin seemed perfectly happy with the way things were, but I couldn't help but to feel bad about a whole list of things. It was his birthday, and he was the one taking me to dinner. I couldn't have afforded a dinner at Tavern on the Green for one, much less for the both of us, and knowing that made me feel like crap.

"Is this your first time here?" Justin asked.

"Are you kidding me?"

Sometimes it threw me how little Justin understood about the way I lived. I looked around the restaurant as the two of us waited for our dinner. The inside was huge and outside there was a patio with even more seating. I liked the chandeliers and the artfully strung lights and as we waited for the waiter to return with our orders I imagined Mike and Melanie having their reception here.

"They have weddings here, don't they?"

"Uhhh, yeah. Why are you asking?"

"I was just thinking about Mike."

"Oh, yeah, right," Justin said. "So when's the big day anyway?"

"They haven't set a date. I think my brother's gonna wait until I graduate since I can't really afford another place right now."

"How many times have I told you I'd help you out?"

"And I told you I'm not letting you pay my rent," I said. "Unless…" I stopped myself from continuing, but it was too late, Justin was going to want to know what I had on my mind.

"Unless what?"

I crossed and uncrossed my ankles, which were thankfully hidden under the table so Justin couldn't see how nervous I was about the question I was about to ask. "I was just thinking, maybe one day, we could get a place together." My face flushed after the words came out. Justin was supposed to be asking me, not the other way around. When I saw the frozen look on his face I immediately regretted opening my big mouth.

"Are you serious?"

"Well, I don't mean right now. I'm just saying at some point."

"I don't know, Jess. I'd love nothing more than to wake up

next to you every morning, but…" Justin shook his head. I waited for an explanation to come, but it didn't.

"You can't live at home forever, Justin."

"Of course, I know that. I just don't think being on my own is something I can consider right now, though."

"Why not? Plenty of amputees live on their own. And you wouldn't really be on your own, you'd have me."

Justin looked at me stone-faced. "Everything is harder for me now, Jess. Just because I don't talk about it doesn't mean it's not real."

"I could help you with those things."

"I don't want to feel like my girlfriend is taking care of me."

"But it's okay for you to try and take care of me? That doesn't seem fair."

"That's different. I'm a guy. I'm supposed to be taking care of you." His face still hadn't softened.

"What are you so afraid is going to happen, anyway?"

"Do we really have to talk about this right now?" I could hear anger edging into Justin's voice. He wasn't the only one getting upset. There was a whole list of things I wanted to say, but I didn't want to start our weekend together fighting, especially because it was Justin's birthday. Still, it was hard to just forget that I'd brought up the idea of moving in together and Justin had basically said no.

I tried tucking my hurt feelings away. When we got to our hotel room I took a shower hoping the hot water would relax me, but alone in the bathroom all I could think about was the conversation I'd had earlier with Justin. There was no way things would work between us if Justin didn't learn to trust me enough to be there for him when things got hard, which made me wonder where our relationship was headed. The rational part of my brain told me that we'd only been together for seven months, and there was no reason to rush things—I'd done that before and wound up regretting it. Eventually Justin would come around and see that I was willing to take the bad with the good, and I wouldn't go running in the opposite direction when things got hard.

By the time I was dressed in my pajamas I felt a little better. Better enough that I was able to paste a smile on my face as I walked out of the bathroom. I would not ruin Justin's birthday, no matter how bruised my ego was.

Justin was sitting up in bed, his back against the headboard. "Can you come here?" he asked. I scooted next to him on the bed. He put his arm around me and kissed the top of my head.

"Lie down," he whispered in my ear.

I looked at him quizzically, not sure what he had in mind.

"Just do it."

I lowered myself down onto my back. "Not that way," Justin said nudging me. I turned over so I was lying on my stomach. He got up and sat beside me, brushed my hair aside with his hand, and kissed the nape of my neck. My body tingled. Justin lifted my shirt over my head so my back was exposed and started to massage my shoulders. His hands were strong and I felt the tension melt away. He kneaded the muscles in my back gently, and when he was done he kissed the spots that his hands had rubbed. When his tongue grazed over my skin I felt goose bumps rising on my flesh. I managed to turn around and then I wrapped my hands around the nape of his neck.

"It's your birthday." I stared into his handsome brown eyes. "I'm supposed to be the one spoiling you."

"I feel spoiled whenever I'm around you." Justin pressed his lips to mine. "Besides, I like making you feel good."

"I know something else you can do to make me feel good," I breathed in his ear. Justin kissed me again.

"So do I." He slid my underwear down and kissed me between my legs.

"Oh, Justin," I moaned and tried to pull him up.

"Not yet, my love." He kept kissing me, over and over in ways I'd never been kissed before until I felt like I'd go crazy if I didn't have him inside me. I stopped worrying about where our relationship was headed. The only thing I thought about was the here and now and how alive and complete I felt when I was with him.

Afterward we lay in each other's arms. Justin stroked the soft pale skin on the inside of my arm. "I don't know how I got to be so lucky." It sounded like he was talking to himself.

"I'm the lucky one."

"No. No you're not." Justin got real quiet after that.

"What's wrong?" I asked. "Why are you so quiet?"

"I'm just thinking."

"About?"

Justin shook his head. "It's nothing important."

I didn't press him to tell me what was on his mind. Instead I looked up at him and smiled and said," I love you."

"I love you too, Jess. I love you, forever."

Chapter 19

In school I'd learned about the Chinese philosophy of yin and yang. It was the first time I'd been able to put a name to the way my life seemed to work. For every high, every happy moment I had, there seemed to be an equally painful and low moment that lurked around the corner and waited for me to let my guard down.

On Sunday afternoon when I turned the key to unlock the door to my apartment and heard music blasting from my brother's room it didn't occur to me that my low was getting itself ready. Even the smell of marijuana wafting into my bedroom from my brother's didn't clue me in. Normally I would have ignored both, but the music was just a bit *too* loud even for me. There was no point in knocking on Mike's door, he wouldn't have heard me. I pushed his door open. He was sitting on his bed, back against the wall, knees bent smoking a joint and bopping his head to the beat of the music he was listening to.

I walked over to the speakers and turned down the volume. "What is going on with you? Are you trying to wake the dead?" I was surprised the neighbors hadn't called the police already.

I knew my brother liked to smoke, and that he liked his music loud, but something about the expression on his face told me there was more going on. I prayed it didn't have to do with Mel, because that would be bad, real bad.

"Same old shit."

"What is that supposed to mean?"

He looked at me square in the face. "It means I'm a stupid piece of shit."

"Oh come on, Mike. You are not."

"Yeah, I am. If you don't believe me, just ask your parents." He held up a letter that was in his hands. "It's all right here."

"What is that?" I asked almost afraid of the answer.

"It's a letter from your dad." By the way he was calling our parents 'your parents' and our father 'your dad' I knew whatever was written on that letter was something I wouldn't like. It was something Mike and I had been doing for years, referring to our parents as yours instead of ours, like neither one of us wanted to claim ownership for either of them. I knew reading the letter Mike held wasn't a good idea, but curiosity got the better of me. I grabbed it out of his hands.

"Why is he writing now anyway?"

"Like I said, I'm an idiot." I stared at my brother, waiting for the real answer. He took another puff from his joint before replying. "I emailed him. I thought he might be interested to know that I'm getting married soon. I even asked if he thought him and Ma could make it for the wedding. Mel really wanted me to try, and so I did, for her…and a little bit for me, too."

"What did he say?"

"You have the letter, read it."

The paper was a bit crumpled. I smoothed it out and looked down at my father's familiar handwriting, and with my heart thumping in my chest, I began to read.

I would like to say it was a pleasure to hear from you and to congratulate you on your upcoming wedding, but I can do neither. For days after receiving your email I asked myself why you bothered to let me into your life again now, and inform me of your news, and then the answer came to me. A wedding needs to be paid for by someone, and why not your parents who you have always viewed as simple and foolish immigrants? Your mother and I struggled for years to do our best to raise you and your sister and provide you with things we never even dreamed of when we were children. What did we get in return, you ask? The answer is nothing. When your mother and I left Croatia we were in search of the American dream, what we wound up with was a nightmare. Insolent, spoiled children who care little for their family is what we ended up with. You think because you are getting married I should be proud of you. Well, I am not. Marriage is a commitment, something you will certainly fail at as you have failed at everything else. I will not be a part of a celebration for a marriage that will go nowhere.

As I told you before your mother and I returned to Croatia, you and Jessica are my biggest disappointments in life. We have no son and no daughter. You are dead to us, and I am formally closing all forms of communication between us. My email address will have changed by the time you receive this letter. My only hope is that one day when you have children of your own they will give you what you have given me and your mother. Unfortunately, I will not be around to see that wish come true.

Regards

"What the fuck is this?" I asked after I finished reading my father's words. Without question I knew they were his. He was always exceptionally good at turning words into weapons even though English wasn't his native language. "You invited him to your wedding? Are you crazy?" My brother was supposed to be smarter than me. How had he expected anything less from our father?

Mike snatched the letter out of my hands. "Great, now my sister thinks I'm a piece of shit, too."

"I do not. You know I love you. But if I wrote a letter to Mom and Dad and got this back you would have told me I was an idiot for expecting anything less."

"I know, I know. I don't know why I let Mel convince me to reach out to them. She just doesn't get it. No one does. No one understands how a mother and a father can just decide they want nothing to do with their own children."

He was right. No one got it. When I lived in the group home people assumed I was there because my parents were drug addicts or alcoholics or something like that. But they weren't, my father was plain crazy, and he and my mother just didn't love me and Mike enough. I sank onto my brother's bed. "Don't let him do this to you, Mike. A wedding is supposed to be good and happy. Don't let Dad take that from you. You know he's messed up in the head."

"Yeah, I do know that. But what I don't know is why it hurts so much."

That was a question I wished I had an answer for, because it wasn't just Mike hurting. It felt like someone was inside my chest piercing my heart with sharp pieces of glass. My father's words were bad enough, but seeing what they were doing to Mike really got to me.

For all the times my parents had hurt me and let me down I should've built a strong enough wall around my heart so nothing they said or did could ever get to me, but a wall like that probably didn't exist. I still remembered like it was yesterday waiting in the courthouse for the family judge to decide on visitation. I'd been living in the group home for a few months and even though I was relieved to be away from my father and thankful that I didn't have to be scared anymore, it hurt that my parents never showed up. They weren't interested in being parents any longer. They'd convinced themselves I was a strung-out teen who was beyond redemption, even though that wasn't even close to being true. I wasn't a perfect child, but I certainly wasn't the devil child my parents made me out to be. A few weeks later I found out my parents had left the country for good. They'd left me and Mike behind without even saying good-bye.

The open bottle of wine on my brother's nightstand called to me. Without even asking for permission I reached for it with a shaky hand and took a few swallows. I was not going to cry. The more I drank, the madder I got. It had been years since I'd had contact with my parents. The last time we talked I'd hoped for an apology from them for how badly they'd hurt me, but that apology never came. They didn't see things the way Mike and I did. To them we were ungrateful spoiled children who defied their parents and showed them no respect. They saw themselves as immigrants who worked themselves to the bone for children who turned out to be failures and disappointments. I couldn't understand how they'd arrived at that version of events. Mike was at the top of his class when he graduated high school, and while I wasn't as smart as Mike, I made good grades in school. Mike didn't experiment with drugs until after my parents decided to leave us behind, and I never had. Sure, sometimes I drank too much, but even that I didn't do very often.

"Promise me you're not going to be writing them any more letters. You know nothing good can come of it," I said, after drinking enough that the hurt was pushed away by the murky feeling that came with too much alcohol.

"Couldn't even if I wanted to. Remember what the letter said. 'I am closing all forms of communication'." My brother's attempt at imitating my father's Croatian accent had me laughing so hard tears started streaming down my face.

"You're such a loser."

"Yeah, well you're a whore."

"And you are not a man, you are just a little boy."

Mike and I hurled insults at each other. The same ones my father did when we were growing up. Somehow turning the hurt into jokes made things better, but that was a lot easier to do when I was goofy from half a bottle of wine.

The next morning I woke up with a splitting headache. It would have bothered me more, but the heavy feeling in my heart distracted me from the throbbing in my head. It took me a minute to remember what was eating at me, and then the memory of reading my brother's letter the day before returned to me. I tried to brush it off as I dressed. I had a class to get to by ten and I didn't need to be distracted by thinking about my father of all people.

My brother had already left for work. There was a note taped to the door of the fridge.

Thanks for making me feel better yesterday J. See you later. Mel's coming over.

I smiled at the thought of a visit from Mel. It felt like forever since I'd seen her. I was almost ready to leave for class when there was a knock on the door. Normally, I wouldn't have answered it. Our next door neighbor had three loser sons who mixed up our door for their dad's all the time. But for some reason I decided to see who it was. I unlocked the door, but left the chain in before opening it. There, standing in the hallway, was Justin's mother. I closed the door to release the chain before opening it again.

"Is Justin okay?" I asked, sure that the only reason she would show up at my door was because something had happened to him. Something bad, because otherwise he would have called me.

"Aren't you going to invite me inside?"

I stepped away from the door. "Of course."

Mrs. Lambert eyed my apartment with poorly hidden disgust.

"How did you know where I live?" I didn't like that she'd just shown up on my front door. The last thing I'd wanted was for her to see my apartment. She probably knew all along that I was a poor college student, but seeing where I lived with her own eyes was confirmation.

"I needed to speak with you alone, so I made it my business to find your address," Mrs. Lambert replied, simply.

I walked over to the table and pulled out a chair. "Do you want to sit?"

"No that's all right. What I came to say shouldn't take very long." Her tone was sharp and I knew whatever was coming I wasn't going to like. "Let's get back to your original question about Justin."

"What question?"

"You asked if Justin was all right—well the answer is no. Justin is not all right. He is not all right at all."

If something was wrong with him, why hadn't he called me? "What happened?"

"What happened is that he thinks he's in love, and he believes you are, too."

I stared at Justin's mother like she had four heads. Who the hell was she to tell me whether or not I loved Justin? "I *do* love him," I said, defensively. Suddenly, I was afraid of the direction our conversation was going to take. I'd been avoiding Justin's mother hoping that it would never come to the type of confrontation she clearly wanted to have.

"You see him as a ticket to your way out of this." Justin's mother swept her hand through the air to indicate that she was talking about my shithole of an apartment. "And I'm here to tell you to stop stringing him along."

"I am not stringing him along." My voice rose. I took a deep breath to calm myself down before continuing. "Look, I know you think I'm only dating him because he has money, but I liked him long before I knew about any of it. He was working at the community center when we met, you know that."

"The two of you are not going to work out, you must see that."

"No, actually, I don't."

"Justin has special needs, needs I seriously doubt you are prepared to help him deal with."

"And why not? I know about his legs, and I know about his PTSD, and I don't care about either one of those things."

"Jessica, you're young and you're pretty and having someone like Justin spoil you with fancy dinners and expensive presents might be fun right now, but what's going to happen when you realize that being with Justin isn't all fun all the time? What's going to happen when he has a complication from his amputation and you have to wheel him around everywhere? What about when he wakes up at night screaming from one of his nightmares? You're just some girl, you're not his family, you don't care for him the way his father and I do."

"You don't get to tell me what my feelings are."

"Jessica…"

"No, wait, you listen to me." I held my hand up and kept talking. "Want to know what I think? I think you keep Justin around as a trophy. You put him up on your mantle to show all your friends that your son is a hero who lost his legs fighting for our country. You want him around because of how it makes you feel, and you don't even bother to take the time out to think about what Justin wants. You should be encouraging him to move out on his own and become independent, but instead you make him think that that's not a possibility for him."

"He needs his family," she replied angrily. "If you cared about him, then you would have insisted he celebrate his birthday with his family instead of pulling him away from us."

"Oh, so that's what this is about. You knew we spent the weekend together and you just couldn't stand it." I couldn't believe the words coming out of Mrs. Lambert's mouth. "He's twenty-six, not six. What grown man do you know would rather hang out with his family on his birthday instead of his girlfriend?"

Mrs. Lambert looked like I'd just slapped her in her face. She was afraid of losing her son to me. I wondered if she'd feel that way if I had a Park Avenue address instead of a Brooklyn one. "You will never fit in with our family, Jessica. The sooner you realize that the better."

"If I told Justin you came out here and said these things to me he'd be so angry with you."

"Yes, he probably would be. But he'll get over it once he realizes how right I am. Eventually Justin will come to accept that his life won't be like his brothers', but it will be okay because he has parents who would do anything for him. Justin's home, his family, is a constant. You are not."

"Newsflash. You and your husband are not going to be around forever. What's gonna happen when the two of you die? Who will take care of him then?"

"We will make the necessary arrangements."

A wave of anger rolled through me. Why did Justin's mother think she had the right to decide his future for him? It was like she'd made up her mind that he was permanently damaged and somehow that meant he wouldn't get to fall in love and get married and have kids the way her other children would. And if he ever did, he wouldn't be doing those things with me, because I wasn't good enough to be a Lambert.

I crossed my arms over my chest. I was done arguing with Justin's mother. There would be no changing her mind, ever. "You said what you came to say, now leave."

Without another word Justin's mother walked out. She

didn't even bother closing the door behind herself, which was fine by me because at least I was able to take some of my anger out on the door as I slammed it shut. I felt like I was in some sort of bizarre soap opera world where rich people did weird things all the time, but it didn't matter because it wasn't real, it was just TV.

I would be late for class because of Justin's mother. It hardly mattered. By the time I got to school I was still so upset that I couldn't concentrate. I sat in the back of the class trying to decide what I was going to do about Justin instead of paying attention to the professor because I was too upset to think straight.

The words from my father's letter and the ones from Justin's mother rang in my head as I made my way home from class later. *A disappointment, dead to me, you won't fit in with our family.* Then I started to think about Justin and how just a few nights earlier he'd told me he didn't want me taking care of him. I'd managed to put it out of my head over the weekend, but with everything that had happened since I last saw him it was hard not to add that to the list of things that were destroying me. By the time I made it home I was on the verge of tears, but I wouldn't let myself cry. Not even my cat curling up in my lap made me feel better. All I could think about was how badly I wanted a do-over, a new life with a normal family and a boyfriend whose parents welcomed me. But there were no do-overs in life.

I picked up the phone and called Susan.

"I really need to get drunk."

"Is that all I'm good for? You need to get drunk, time to call Susan."

"I'm sorry." It was all I managed to get out before I choked on the tears that began to slide down my face.

"Hey, I was just kidding. Of course you can come over."

"No." My common sense was trying to override my emotions. "I got drunk yesterday. It's probably not a good idea for me to do it again."

"What's wrong? Did you and Justin get into a fight?"

"No. It's a long story. Just forget I called."

"I can't just forget. You sound awful, Jesse. I'm coming over."

She hung up before I could talk her out of it. A few minutes later Mike and Mel showed up, by then I had wiped my eyes.

"We're getting pizza," Mel announced as I walked into the kitchen to greet her. Normally I loved getting pizza with Mel because she was the only person I knew who loved thin crust with jalapenos as much as I did, but not even pizza was going to get me out the funk I was in.

"What's up with you?" Mike asked. "You're not still thinking about that stupid letter, are you? I'm totally over it, and you should be, too."

"It's not that." I shook my head. "Well, maybe it is a little."

"Then what's wrong?"

"What if Mel's family hated you? What if they didn't want you and her to be together?"

"Is this about Justin and his mother?"

"Yeah. She came over today…"

"Wait a minute. She showed up here? At the apartment?"

"Yup."

"Why?"

"To tell me she doesn't believe that I love Justin, and that I don't fit in with their family."

"Oh my God!" Mel said. "I would've slapped that bitch in her face."

"Believe me, I thought about it. But I don't think Justin would be very happy with me if I did."

"Did you tell him what she said?"

"No, and I don't think I'm going to either."

There was a knock on the door. Susan. I let her in.

"So, are you going to tell me what's going on?" she asked as she looked at all our faces.

"Her boyfriend's mother hates her," Mike chimed in.

I told Susan the story about Mrs. Lambert's visit. She also thought I needed to tell Justin, but I was afraid his mother was right. I was afraid that he might be angry with her at first, but eventually he would forgive her, and I'd feel even more left out of his family than I already did. I didn't want him to have to choose between me and his family, because I was pretty sure he wouldn't pick me.

"What am I going to do?" I wondered if Mike knew how lucky he had it. Mel's family treated him like he belonged, and that probably made up for the fact that our mother and father couldn't give a shit about us.

"You're not going to do anything," Susan said. "She can't tell you what to do. Fuck her."

Mike was looking at me, his eyes full of sympathy. "Look, J, I hate to say this, but the choice is pretty simple."

"And that would be?"

"You and I don't know what it means to have a real family, but I know that's what you want. I've seen you do some stupid shit to try and get it, too."

Leave it to my brother to come right out and say something like that. "Like what?"

"Like move in with that loser who was boning some girl behind your back."

I rolled my eyes at Mike and put my hands on my hips. "Gee, thanks for reminding me."

"The point is, Justin can't give you what you want. He might make you happy now, but sooner or later that train's gonna come to a stop, and you're gonna have to hop off."

"Mike," Mel snapped.

"Hey, I'm just being honest here."

Because that's what Mike did. He told the truth whether you liked hearing it or not, and a small part of me worried that he was right. What I didn't know was how I was ever going to find the courage to hop off the train before it crashed and left me in a million pieces.

"I brought up the idea of moving in together to Justin."

"What did he say?" asked Susan, sounding surprised. I could understand why. It was just over a year ago that I vehemently swore I'd never move in with a guy again. But Justin was different.

"That he didn't want his girlfriend taking care of him."

"That's such bullshit," Mel interrupted. "That's what you do when you're a couple, you take care of each other."

"I'm sorry, Mike. I know if it was up to you you'd be on the next plane to Vegas with Mel instead of helping me make rent here."

"Don't even say the V word. Especially not around my family."

"Mel's family would kill us both if we didn't have a wedding that included her whole *entire* family," my brother said, dramatically. "And that's gonna take at least a year to plan."

"At least," agreed Mel.

"Don't worry, J." Mike rubbed my shoulder with his hand. "I won't leave you hanging."

Chapter 20

When I woke up the next morning it dawned on me that the night before had been the first that I hadn't spoken to Justin since we'd started dating. I picked up my phone and realized that somehow I'd turned off the ringer. There were a lot of missed calls from Justin, but he hadn't left any messages and he was probably already at work so I didn't want to bother him. I slumped out of bed and figured by the time he got off of work I'd have my head together enough to talk to him. Somehow I was able to make it through all three classes I had that day even though it was always there—that sinking feeling in my chest and the 'you're not good enough' voice in my head.

I dragged myself back home, so lost in how bad I felt that I didn't even notice Justin sitting on the stoop in front of my building until I practically stumbled over him.

"What are you doing here?" I was so surprised to see him. Then his mother's visit came back to me and I worried he'd come to tell me something I didn't want to hear. Maybe she'd convinced him I was all wrong for him and he was here to tell me.

Justin stood and I looked in his eyes. There were dark circles under them. "I came to see if you were all right and you obviously are, so I'll just go now."

Justin started to walk away. I grabbed his hand. "Hey, wait. Where are you going?"

"What do you care?" he replied, his voice heavy with anger.

"Justin? Why are you mad at me?"

He turned around to face me, but didn't answer right away. "I haven't heard from you since you said goodbye to me on Sunday. Which means one of two things, and since you're obviously okay and not lying in a hospital bed somewhere, then the only reason you haven't called is because you don't have the courage to tell me to my face that you're done with me."

"*What* are you talking about?"

"If you changed your mind about me, you could've at least told me." Justin's voice rose. "I was up all night waiting to hear from you."

"You got it all wrong. I had my ringer off. Mike and Mel were home and Susan came over and I got distracted. I'm sorry."

Justin remained stone-faced. Had he really thought I was avoiding him? Just a few days ago we'd both said I love to you each other. Did he really have so little faith in me that he'd think I could tell him I love you one day and want to break up with him the next? I rested my hand on his arm. "Justin, c'mon. I'm sorry."

"Don't do that to me again." His voice cracked, it sounded like he was trying to choke back tears.

"Hey, come here." I pulled him into my arms. His body was stiff. I didn't like what he'd been thinking, but seeing him so upset was even worse. "I'm sorry."

"I swore I wouldn't do this to you. I swore if you decided you didn't want to be with me that I'd let you go, no questions asked, but I don't think I can, Jess."

"I'm here, Justin, and I don't want you to let me go. I'm sorry about last night." Justin began to relax in my arms as my words sunk in.

He held my face in his hands and stared into my eyes before pressing his lips on mine. He kissed me like I was his air and laced his hands through my hair. Everything melted away except for the feel of his hands touching me. "Can we go inside?"

"Mmmm."

It was hard to stop kissing him, but I managed to pull myself away and get the door unlocked. Inside my apartment Justin pinned me against the wall and kissed me again. I could tell what he wanted and I needed him as badly as he needed me so I was willing to risk the embarrassment of my brother walking in on us. Layers of clothing came off, falling on the floor as the two of us made our way to my bedroom. We lay beside each other and when Justin entered me I inhaled sharply. My heart raced and that dizzy feeling I always had when Justin and I were close came over me. I pulled his face towards mine and kissed him. His hips moved in rhythm with mine, he was both gentle and urgent at the same time until he held on to me tightly as he spasmed with pleasure.

We lay silently beside each other after. There were no windows in my bedroom so there was no way for me to tell how late it was getting. Justin kissed the top of my head and I lifted my head to look at him.

"I can't believe you actually thought I was breaking up with you," I finally said.

"We talk every day, Jess. And then out of the blue I don't hear from you for two days." Justin eased me off his chest and sat up. "You can deny it all you want, but I know you were upset with me this weekend."

"You were upset, too."

"Not with you, though. I was mad at myself."

"For what?"

"For not being the perfect man you deserve."

"Justin, you have to stop that already."

"I'm sorry. I can't help the way I feel." I inched closer to Justin and he draped his arm on my shoulder. "You told me what happened Monday, but why didn't you call after you got back home on Sunday?"

I didn't want to think about the letter Mike showed me, much less talk about it. "It's a long story."

"So we're back to that now?"

"Back to what?"

"You not telling me things."

I lowered my eyes. "Mike got a letter from my dad. It was really hard to read it—and to see my brother that upset. We both had a little too much to drink after."

"What did the letter say?"

"Mike told him that he was getting married and that he wanted him and my mother to come to the wedding, but my father said no, and that as far as he was concerned we were dead to him."

"Oh my God, Jess." Justin pulled me closer to him and wrapped one of his arms around me. "Now I feel like a jerk for getting mad at you. I'm sorry. Your dad's an asshole. How can he not see how awesome you and your brother are?"

"It doesn't matter. To be honest, I don't really want to think about it anymore."

Being in Justin's arms was comforting and it helped me to forget things I didn't like thinking about. I wanted him to spend the night, but I wouldn't ask him to do that. He couldn't sleep with his prosthetic legs on, and it would be impossible for him to get in and out of the shower in my apartment without them. It was late when Justin left and I hated watching him go because after he was gone I knew I wouldn't be able to stop myself from thinking about all the things I was too afraid to mention to him.

Chapter 21

Midterm exams came and went. They were a good excuse for not having a lot of time to talk, but after they were done I couldn't think of a reason to cut my nightly conversations with Justin short. It wasn't that I didn't like talking to him, but every conversation took my mind to things I hated thinking about. I watched Mike and Mel together and knew I'd never have what they did. Mike had a family with her, which was something I'd never have with Justin. I swore to Mike and even to Justin that my father's words didn't matter to me, but it was a lie. I tried convincing myself that Justin's mother was wrong for telling me everything she had told me, but I was fooling myself. Every time I looked at my reflection in the mirror I remembered her words. *You don't fit.* She was wrong about my feelings for Justin, but she was right about everything else. From the time Justin and I shared a cab and I saw the building he lived in I should've convinced myself that I wasn't right for him. If he hadn't been injured, would he ever have been interested in a girl like me? I couldn't help but wonder if he lowered his standards because he didn't think he could do better than someone like me. Maybe that was the real reason he didn't want to move out of his parent's house and in with me.

It was April and most of the students in my classes were doing the spring break thing. Justin and I were spending our Sunday together like we almost always did. We stopped by a coffee shop, brought our lattes to the park near my apartment, and sat beside each other on a bench. Justin threw out some crumbs for the pigeons.

"You better be careful or we'll get swarmed," I warned him.

Just then a pigeon flew over Justin's head and its droppings landed on his shoulder. I laughed while Justin tried to wipe his shirt.

"They say it's supposed to be good luck."

"Oh, really?" He looked at me when he was done cleaning his shirt. "Since I've got all this supposed good luck all of a sudden then I should ask you what I want to ask you before it disappears."

My heart beat a little faster. I had no idea what he was going to ask, but I knew what I wanted him to.

"What is it?" I took a sip of my coffee.

"I was hoping for another weekend together."

Another weekend. That wasn't enough for me anymore. I braced myself for what I was about to say and lowered my gaze. "I don't think so." It was impossibly hard telling him no. I always wanted to give him everything he wanted, but what about what I wanted?

Justin furrowed his brow. "Why not?" he asked, confused by my response.

"How long are we going to keep doing this?"

"Doing what?"

"Sneaking off to hotel rooms," I said blankly. "It's just not the way normal couples do things."

"I didn't realize you felt that way." Justin turned to face me and rested his hand on my knee. "But from the beginning you knew we weren't exactly a normal couple. And I've told you a million times I don't mind staying at your place, but you're so hung up about it."

"Because I don't want my brother walking in on us, and my apartment is disgusting. You know that."

"We don't have to do anything. You know I'm fine just being with you."

"If that's the case, why is it that I can't come to your house?"

"You can come over anytime you like. You're the one who doesn't want to."

"It's not like I don't have a reason. Your mother hates my guts, she doesn't want the two of us together. How am I supposed to spend time around someone who feels that way about me?"

"I told you..."

"Yes, yes, yes, you told me she'd get over it eventually once I was done kissing her ass." A shocked looked passed over Justin's face. I was upset and not hiding it very well. "But you're wrong. I heard what she said about me on Christmas Eve, she thinks I'm after your money. She doesn't like me, and that's never going to change."

"What do you mean you heard what she said on Christmas Eve?"

"Do you remember that I told you that night that I got cold so I went back to your place without Jeff?" Justin nodded. "Well,

I got back a lot earlier than you thought I did. I heard you arguing with your mother behind the door."

My confession caught Justin by surprise. "Why didn't you tell me?"

"For what? What difference would it have made? You live with your mother, you need her, and she's the one you trust to take care of you, not me."

"That's not how it is." Justin reached for my hand. I let him hold it but I couldn't bring myself to look into his eyes as he spoke. "I've told my mother plenty of times that I love you and that you're a part of my life, but I can always talk to her again."

"No! You don't get it. Your mother HATES me. She practically told me herself the day after your birthday."

"The day after my birthday? What are you talking about?"

"She came over…"

"To your house?"

I nodded. "Yes. She was angry at me that you decided to spend the weekend with me and skip your party. She doesn't believe that I really love you, she thinks I'm only interested in your money. Your mother told me I'd never fit into your family."

"Those were her exact words?" I nodded and Justin's eyes widened in anger, he stood up and walked a few paces away before turning around to face me. "Why are you only telling me this now?"

"Because I knew it wouldn't make a difference," I said with my voice raised. Weeks of pent up emotions came rolling out. "Your mother was right. You might be mad at her now, but you won't stay mad, because you don't believe in me enough to stand up to her."

"That's not true."

I thought I was doing so well until I felt a tear make its way down my cheek. I lowered my head, not wanting Justin to see.

"Justin, don't you see how messed up this is for me? I've told you more than once how badly it hurts that I don't have a family. And no matter what I do, no matter how hard I try, I'll never have one with you. Can't you at least try and understand how much that hurts?"

Justin shoved his hands into his pockets. "I can't control my mother. It's not fair that you're blaming me for what she said to you."

I stood up and walked over to Justin collecting my thoughts along the way. "I could deal with knowing your mother hates me, I could deal with the fact that she doesn't want us being together. If we wanted to, we could make our own family and it wouldn't matter what anyone thought, except…"

"Except what?"

"You don't trust me enough for that to happen. I've waited and waited for you to believe in me the way two people who love each other are supposed to, but I feel like you don't want to let me get any closer to you."

Justin's head snapped up and his eyes bore into me. "Jessica, what is this really all about?"

"What do you mean, what is this about?"

"You're inventing problems that don't exist because you can't let me be right. I told you last summer this would happen, that you'd get tired of dating a cripple, I knew it, and you insisted that I was wrong."

"Are you saying that everything I just told you I made up?"

"I've let you get closer to me than I ever planned on, Jess. What more is it that you want from me?"

"I want you to tell your mother that everything she said about me was wrong. I want you to tell her that you and I plan on being together for a very long time, and if she can't accept that then too bad because you don't need her to take care of you when you have me."

"What you're asking is impossible and you know it."

"Why is it impossible?"

"You know why," Justin practically yelled at me. Then he shook his head. "Don't pin this on my mother. I know she's said some awful things about you, but if you changed your mind about me then at least have the courage to come out and say it."

Not this again. I was shocked by Justin's words. I tried to think of some way to respond, but I couldn't.

"You've been different ever since our last weekend together. I thought it was the letter you told me about from your dad, but maybe there was no letter, maybe you were lying to me about that, too."

"Justin." I couldn't believe what I was hearing. "I haven't lied to you, ever."

"But you've kept things from me, haven't you? Things you knew could ruin our relationship, things you could use as excuses to back out of being with me. Because this," Justin yanked up one leg of the track pants he was wearing and pointed to his artificial limb, "turned out to be more than you wanted to deal with."

I was too angry to be kind. Heat filled my chest and I felt ready to explode. "It always comes down to the same thing with you. You didn't want to date me because you thought I was too shallow to care for you. Then you finally agreed, and now I can't help but to wonder why. You may not have your legs, but you're still a man and you have needs after all. Maybe that's all I was to you. Good enough to take to a hotel for the weekend, but not for more."

Justin's phone rang. He pulled it out of his pocket and without even glancing down to see who was calling he threw it hard and fast until it landed several yards away shattered and useless.

"What the hell did you do that for?"

Justin turned around and stared at me icily. "You don't want me calling you anymore, do you? Well, now I won't be able to."

"Justin, I…"

"No." He held his hand up to me. "Don't say anything else."

"Justin, please." Tears were streaming down my face uncontrollably. I felt bad for what I'd said, I wanted to believe it was all wrong, but a small voice kept asking *what if you're not.* I prayed Justin would tell me he loved me and that I wasn't right, but instead he began to walk away.

For a few moments I stared at him still not believing what had just transpired. Then I ran after him and stopped a few feet away. "Justin, can't we just talk about this?"

He ignored me and kept walking. I wanted to follow him and beg him to listen, but my pride wouldn't let me.

"Son of a bitch," he yelled and then made a fist and rammed it into a tree that lined the street just outside of the entrance to the park. I'd seen Justin upset, but never like this. I wasn't sure what hurt more, him walking away from me, or knowing that he was also in pain. But his pain blinded him to the fact that other people had feelings. All he could see was himself as this broken person no one could ever love, and he didn't care what that did to me.

When Justin was long gone, and I was sure he wouldn't turn around to come find me, I managed to choke in a breath of air even though my chest felt so tight. Somehow I made my way back home.

For a long time I sat on my bed in a daze, not really quite understanding what had just happened. I waited and waited for a call from Justin, but none came. I curled into a ball and began to cry again. All I could think was that Justin and I couldn't be over, there was just no way.

Chapter 22

For days I walked around in a fog. I cried myself to sleep at night and woke up with dark circles under my eyes. In the park on the last day I'd seen Justin, he told me he wasn't going to call me, and he made good on that promise. Not a single call or text. It was like he'd dropped off the face of the earth. I thought about calling him and telling him I just wanted to make sure he was all right, but what if he didn't want to talk to me? I'd rather not hear his voice at all than hear it tell me he didn't want anything to do with me.

April turned into May and I poured myself into studying for finals. I stayed at school late studying with my classmates who didn't seem to mind that all of a sudden I'd taken an interest in the study groups they'd been inviting me to all semester long. At home, I practically hid from my brother so I wouldn't have to answer any of his questions about Justin. But one Saturday morning after I returned from the laundromat my brother was home and in the kitchen and before I had a chance to run into my bedroom he stopped me.

"It feels like forever since we talked."

"I've just been busy with school."

"And Justin," my brother teased.

I put my bag of laundry down on the floor. I hesitated before answering, first combing through my mind to decide whether or not I could tell my brother about our break-up without breaking down and crying like a baby.

"There is no me and Justin anymore."

My brother stopped what he was doing and looked at me. "You're serious?"

"Yup."

"What the fuck happened?" My brother asked sounding more surprised than I thought he would. He's the one who'd told me months ago he didn't think our relationship was on solid ground.

I sighed and pulled out a chair from under the kitchen table. "We had a huge fight. I told him about the things his mother said and he claimed I was using it as an excuse to break up with him because I can't deal with him being an amputee and I didn't have the courage to be honest with him."

"That's such bullshit."

"It doesn't matter what it is. I haven't heard from Justin since the day we had that fight."

"When did all this happen?"

"Spring break."

"Spring break? Why didn't you tell me?"

"Because I didn't know how." I looked up at my brother. "I feel like a total loser."

"J, c'mon. You're not a loser. And you know I liked Justin, but after what he went through I can't really blame him for being a little messed up in the head."

"Yeah, well. It is what it is." I stood up, pushed my chair back under the table and picked up my laundry from the floor. "I gotta put these clothes away."

My brother didn't ask me any more questions about Justin after that. He knew me well enough to know it wasn't what I wanted to talk about.

That night I lay in bed wondering if Justin thought about me at all. I'd gone from feeling hurt to feeling angry. He said he loved me, how could he just let go of what we had so easily? Maybe the reason he didn't defend me to his mother more than he had was because he thought she was right, that I was only interested in his money. Maybe that was a trade he was okay with. My companionship in exchange for dinners and gifts. The thought made my stomach turn and I began to question if what we had was ever real.

One morning while I got ready for class I found myself staring at my reflection in the mirror, *not good enough,* it said to me. It was amazing how quickly I'd gone from being the happiest I remembered to not even being able to look at myself. My ringing phone interrupted my self-pity. I looked down at it to see who was calling. Justin's brother, Jeff. For a second I thought about not answering, but I couldn't let it go to voicemail, I had to know to know what he wanted to talk to me about.

"Hello."

"Jessica?"

"Yeah? What's up? Is Justin okay?" I couldn't think of any other reason he would call me.

"He's not okay, but it's very sweet of you to ask since you're the reason." Jeff's raised voice was filled with sarcasm.

"How am I the reason? Justin is the one who walked away from me, not the other way around," I said defensively.

Jeff hesitated before replying. "That's not exactly how he tells it."

"What did he tell you?"

"He said you were done with him—that you couldn't deal with all his issues and that you weren't even brave enough to tell him the truth so you made some half-assed excuse to break things off with him." Jeff paused. "I thought you were different, Jesse. I even swore to my mom that you were."

"That's *not* what happened."

"Then tell me what did, because I just don't get this."

"I don't even know where to begin." I sighed. "We got into a big fight. Justin wanted to spend the weekend together and I told him no."

"Why?"

None of this was any of Jeff's business, but I answered him anyway. I felt like I needed to get it off my chest. "Did Justin tell you that I asked him if he wanted to move in together?"

"No," Jeff replied, sounding genuinely surprised.

"Well, I did. And he said no. Do you want to know why?"

"Yeah."

"He doesn't want me to be the one who helps him through whatever happened to him in Afghanistan. He has your mother for that, your mother who hates me. And I just couldn't deal with wondering if Justin will *ever* love me or trust me enough for us to have more than an occasional weekend together."

"And that's what you told him?"

"It's what I tried to tell him. But he wouldn't listen. He got it into his head that I didn't want to be with him, and I was using your mother as an excuse to break up with him."

"Because that's what he really thinks. *Damn,*" Jeff swore under his breath. "I don't know what to do. Justin's a mess. My mom called a few days after you two broke up and told me to come back home. Justin smashed up his room and locked himself in and she couldn't get him to come out."

"Jeff, I'm so sorry."

"Do you still love my brother?"

"I do," I said practically choking on the words. "I don't think I'll ever stop."

"He was a different person after the two of you started dating, did you know that? After everything that happened in Afghanistan, he was so depressed. He hardly ever left the house because he was so embarrassed about his legs. Then he started working at the community center and he seemed better, but you were the one who brought the light back into his eyes. Without you, it's gone again."

A tear slid down my cheek. I ached for Justin. "What am I supposed to do?"

"Can you call him?"

And then what? "If Justin can't bring himself to trust me and believe in me, then it'll never work between us. I get it that's he's hurting, but I am, too."

"I'm sorry. I know you're right. It's just that ever since Justin and his ex-fiancee broke up, he's convinced himself that no girl could ever want him the way he is now."

"Even after being together for almost a year he still believed that about me. I could call him now and convince him to take me back, but he won't trust me now any more than he did before." I loved Justin with all my heart, still did, but it hurt knowing he didn't believe it. Every cell in my body was shouting at me to call Justin, to find a way back to him, but then what? All of our problems would still be there and when we got over the high of being back in each other's arms they would just rear their ugly heads again.

"You know I have a ton of my own issues so I'm the last person who should be judging anyone else, but I think what Justin really needs is to go back to counseling," I said.

"At least you and my mother agree on something. The problem is, Justin doesn't." Jeff let out a sigh. "I don't know what to do, but I'll figure something out. I'm sorry I yelled at you, Jesse."

"It's fine. I get it, you love your brother."

"For what it's worth, the rest of us Lamberts really liked you. James and my dad, they thought you and Justin were the perfect fit."

So did I.

For the next few days after my conversation with Jeff, I held on to the hope that he'd talked to Justin and somehow convinced him that the two of us were worth fighting for. After a week passed I let that hope go, and mourned the end of me and Justin again. Towards the end of May the scar left behind by my break-up with Justin was still so raw that when Mrs. Connor called to ask if I wanted to work at the community center again over the summer I had to tell her no, even though I wanted to, badly, but the idea of seeing Justin every day and not being able to touch him and hold him and kiss him was too hard. Instead, I settled for a job waiting tables at a small restaurant a few blocks from my apartment. With tips it actually paid better than what I had made last summer, but I hated it, especially on weekend nights when the bar filled up with a bunch of drunk idiots.

~

Every day seemed the same. It had been almost three months without Justin, and I still felt lost and broken. Each morning I woke up telling myself that things would get better, but as the days rolled by, I wasn't sure that was true anymore.

"Why is what I want out of a relationship more important than what Justin wants?" I asked my brother one morning, a rare one when he was actually around. I still second-guessed my decision not to call Justin all the time. I missed him so much that I was almost willing to go back to the way things were and accept that as my future. At least Justin was in it somewhere.

"Who said it was?" My brother turned to face me, coffee mug in hand. He lifted it to his lips and took a sip before continuing. "The thing is, Justin has the same right to demand from you what he wants as you do, but neither of you is obliged to give it. I think the couples that wind up working out are the ones who are okay with each other's wants."

"How the hell did you get to be so smart?"

"Believe it or not, I've been where you are before, wanting something from someone that they just couldn't give."

"Oh really? Does Mel know about that?"

"Yeah. We talk about our old relationships, it's better than pretending that no one existed before we met each other."

"And you don't get jealous?"

"I kind of do, sometimes, but I don't think Mel does. She knows she's the only one for me." My brother gulped down the last bit of his coffee before setting his cup down on the kitchen counter. "I wish I could stay and talk some more, but I really gotta get going, or I'll be late for work."

"Hey, before you go, I need a favor."

"What's up?"

"There's this book I need for one of my fall classes and they don't have it at my school's bookstore but they have it at yours…"

"And you want me to pick it up for you?"

"Actually I was thinking that maybe we can meet over by Hunter and get lunch together sometime this week?"

"What about today? I can meet you at around one."

"Okay."

I didn't have to be at work until four thirty so at least it gave me something to do. I wound up at the meeting spot my brother and I had decided on almost a half hour early. There was no shade to be had and it was crazy hot outside. So hot that I decided to duck into a nearby air-conditioned store and pretend I was actually going to buy something, but then I heard my name being called. I turned to see who it was.

I was surprised to see Jeff jogging towards me. He greeted me with a hug.

"What are you doing around here?" I asked.

Jeff looked at me like the answer was obvious. "I don't live that far from here."

"Yeah, right. I know that." For some reason I'd blocked that piece of information from my head. But it was a weekday, which meant Justin was at work, so there was no chance of running into him.

"How's Justin doing?"

"He's better, I think. After I spoke to you Justin and I had a talk. Or at least I talked and he listened. I didn't think anything I said really made much of a difference until my mom called me a few weeks after to tell me Justin was moving out."

"What?" I wasn't sure I'd heard him right. "Justin's getting his own place?"

"Already did, he was able to find a handicapped friendly apartment and moved last week."

"That's great," I said, trying my best to muster a smile. I wanted to be happy for Justin. He clearly was doing a much better job moving on with his life than I was. "I'm glad he's doing well."

I stared down at my feet. Jeff reached for my arm and I looked back up at him. "He's better, but he's not the same. The light in his eyes hasn't come back. I really think you're the only thing that can make that happen."

I shook my head. "I don't think so. He hasn't called, not even once since he walked away from me."

"He's waiting."

"Waiting for what?"

"To be the man you want him to be."

"What do you mean?"

"You had faith in him. At least that's what he told me. He said that's why he was moving out, because you believed he could do it, and, if you believed in him then he owed it to you to believe in himself."

"He really said that?"

Jeff nodded, "Yeah."

From the corner of my eye I spotted my brother approaching. "Sorry I'm late, J," he said as he came to stand beside me.

Jeff glared at my brother. It took me a second to realize what he was thinking.

"Umm, Jeff, this is my brother, Mike." I turned to look at Mike who'd stuck his hand out and was shaking Jeff's. "This is Justin's brother, Jeff."

"Nice to meet you," Jeff said, looking relieved. Maybe Justin was over us, but it seemed like Jeff still had hope that the two of us would get back together. "You guys do kind of look alike," he commented.

"You ready, J?" My brother asked. "I have to be back at work in an hour."

"Yeah. Let's go." I turned to give Jeff a kiss on his cheek. "Tell Justin I said hi."

"You should tell him yourself."

For days after my run in with Justin's brother I thought about what he'd said, but I couldn't bring myself to pick up the phone. I was glad Justin was on his own, but I worried about him being okay. We'd known each other for almost a year, but I still didn't know that much about his day-to-day life at home. I'd seen him put on his prosthetic limbs once or twice, but that was about the extent of things. It wasn't that I didn't want to know, Justin was always so guarded about the whole thing that every time I asked him a question I felt like I was crossing a line and intruding where I wasn't welcome.

The weekend came and I stopped by Susan's for a movie night.

She'd gotten absurdly nauseating to spend time around since she and Greg had gotten engaged. They were getting married in October, and every conversation seemed to revolve around wedding plans. Truthfully, I was happy for her, but hearing her gush about her boyfriend made me miss Justin more than I already did.

"What's with you?" She tossed a popcorn at me. "You're quieter than usual."

"I'm just thinking."

"About what?" I shot her a knowing look. "Yeah, right." She rolled her eyes. "Why did I bother asking? Justin is all you *ever* think about."

"He is not," I protested before explaining myself. "It's just that I ran into his brother a few days ago."

"Really?" Susan's eyes widened. "What did he tell you?"

"That Justin moved out, he's got his own apartment now." I hesitated before continuing worried about what Susan would say. "He also said the light in Justin's eyes hasn't come back, and he thinks I'm the only one that can make that happen."

"Okay, that's pretty cheesy, but if it's true, Jesse, I really think that maybe you should call him. I mean the main problem you had was wondering if he was going to stay at home and let his mother take care of him forever."

"That wasn't exactly the main problem. The main problem was wondering if he would ever trust me enough to leave home and let *me* be the one to help him when he needs it."

"Well, you're halfway there."

"Justin finally believing in himself is huge, but just because he was able to do that, it doesn't mean he'll be able to believe in me, too."

"But you won't know if you don't try."

Hanging out with Susan had been a bad idea, I decided. Because, truthfully, all I needed was a push—not even a push, only the slightest nudge in Justin's direction to break my resolve. I should've kept quiet about my run-in with Jeff, but it's all I thought about that week and keeping it inside made thinking about anything else damn near impossible.

Chapter 23

By Monday I realized I had no other choice but to take a chance and talk to Justin. And it couldn't be over the phone, I had to see him in person. Maybe nothing would come of it, but I needed some kind of closure. Even though I'd been at work since close to midnight the night before, I got up early, put on the cutest sundress in my closet and hopped on the train. I stood in the shade of the community center's awning waiting for a taxi to pull up and let Justin out. It felt like my heart was in my throat. I waited and waited. Taxi after taxi drove by, but none actually stopped. I began to wonder if Justin was ever going to show up, and then I heard my name being called.

"Jess." I couldn't bring myself to turn my head in Justin's direction. He walked towards me. "Jess, what are you doing here?"

I felt like I couldn't breathe. The last time I'd seen him he'd been so angry. His face was softer now, but I couldn't read his thoughts. "You're walking?" I said. Why had I let those be the first words out of my mouth?

"Yeah, well I haven't learned how to fly yet."

"But you always take a taxi."

"Not anymore." Justin paused before continuing. "You were right about a lot of things, Jess. There were so many things I was too afraid to do, but taking the subway turns out to be no big deal." I smiled. Justin looked the same, but something about him seemed so different. "And since I've got my own apartment now and have to pay rent, I figured I should be a little more careful about spending money."

"You look good, Justin. I'm happy for you," I said, my voice barely above a whisper.

"I thought you'd be more surprised about my news."

"I ran into Jeff last week, he told me you moved out on your own."

"Hmmm. He didn't tell me."

"I don't want to make you late for work." I looked into Justin's eyes then turned away. It was hard to be that close to him when I knew we were no longer an "us." "I just wanted to see you, and make sure you were okay, and ask you if you think maybe one day we can at least be friends." Thoughts of Justin happy with another girl flooded my mind out of nowhere. I shook my head trying to clear the image. It would be near impossible to be friends with him. "I'm sorry. I probably should have just called."

"Then why didn't you?"

I was afraid he wouldn't answer. So instead I'd gotten on a train and ridden an hour to make sure I'd have a chance to talk to him, but I hadn't taken into account the way he'd make me feel standing so close to him, even though he was still so out of reach. "I'm off today, didn't have anything else to do."

"Jess." Justin waited for me to look at him again before continuing. "I've missed you." He reached for my hand and laced his fingers through mine. I felt faint as my heart flip-flopped in my chest. I wanted to say something to let Justin know that I missed him, too, but I couldn't find the words. Instead I stared at my feet. Justin tilted my chin up, forcing me to meet his eyes. "I was sort of hoping the reason you came all the way up here was because you missed me, too."

I nodded ever so slightly, but enough for Justin to notice. He leaned towards me and before I knew what was happening he pressed his lips softly on mine. My breath caught in my throat. I dropped Justin's hand and wrapped my arms around him.

"I was scared you still hated me," I finally said.

"I never hated you." My head rested on Justin's chest as he spoke. "It wasn't really you I was angry at that day, but myself. I'm still really ashamed about the way I acted."

"Justin, I…"

Before I had a chance to finish what I was going to say Justin dropped his arms from around me and grabbed my hand leading me behind him into the community center.

"Where are we going?"

"You said you were off today, didn't you?"

"Yes, but…"

We passed by Don who was sitting in front at his desk. "Jessica, what are you doing here?" he asked.

I would've answered, but Justin pulled me past him before I had a chance. We finally stopped in front of Mrs. Connor's office. Justin knocked on her door and after she told us come in we walked inside.

"Oh, Jessica. What a lovely surprise," she said before turning to Justin. "What's up, Justin?"

"I'm going to need the day off."

Mrs. Connor smiled, her eyes darted back and forth between me and Justin. "If it was anyone else…"

"Thanks." Justin gave her a hug and I stifled an urge to laugh at the surprised look on her face. "You're the best."

I followed Justin out of the building and back onto the street. "Where are we going?"

"You decide. I don't really care, I just want to be with you."

"I don't know." I hadn't expected Justin to take the day off to spend it with me. I half believed that he wouldn't even agree to talk to me so my mind still felt like it needed to catch up to what was happening.

"We have a lot to talk about, Jess. And I'd like to do that somewhere private." He hesitated before continuing. "Can I take you to my place?"

I nodded, still somewhat in a daze. I couldn't believe I was holding Justin's hand again, much less that we were on our way to his apartment.

Justin hailed a taxi. "I thought you were done with cabs," I teased as we settled in beside each other.

"I don't want to wait a second longer to get you alone than it has to."

Justin's apartment was a bit farther from the community center than where he'd lived before, but it was still in Manhattan. The apartment was spacious and updated, and, despite the fact that it was barely furnished, it was still a million times nicer than mine.

"Do you want anything to drink?" Justin asked as I took a seat on the couch.

"A glass of water would be nice."

I looked around while Justin poured me some water from a pitcher in his refrigerator. He walked over and handed me the glass. "I haven't been here that long. I'm planning on getting more furniture soon."

"So what made you finally decide to do it, to get your own place?"

Justin sat beside me. "After that fight we had I was really angry, and then I got really, really depressed. I was so sure I was right about the things I said to you in the park that day until Jeff barged into my room one day and told me I was being an ass and that I'd just run off the best thing that had ever happened to me. He told me he'd talked to you, and he was really pissed at me for walking away from you, and then coming home and acting like you'd been the one who dumped me. I was really mad at first, but after a few days I began to think about the things Jeff said, and I started seeing your side of things." Justin lowered his head like he was afraid to look in my eyes. I reached for his hand. "I was so sure that you couldn't—that no one could—love someone like me that I never really let you in. I was too busy thinking about the problems in my life to realize that I was hurting you. And I'm sorry for doing that."

"I'm sorry I didn't try harder to understand."

Justin shook his head. "It wouldn't have mattered. In case you haven't noticed I can be kind of stubborn."

I tried not to laugh. "Yeah, I've noticed."

"Anyway, it took me a while, but bit by bit, I started getting my head together, and then I wasn't angry anymore—I just missed you like crazy. I wanted to find you and beg you to forgive me and take me back. I even came to your neighborhood a few times, but I always turned back around. I swore that when I saw you again, when I asked you to forgive me, that I'd have my shit together and be the man you deserved. That's when I decided to look for my own place. Because you were right." Justin smiled, his amber eyes lit up. "I'm starting to believe you're always right."

"No, I am *so* not."

"I have challenges, but I'm not a cripple. I'm actually really lucky. There's tons of guys who got hurt way worse than I did, but instead of being grateful for still being able to walk, I just felt sorry for myself." Justin spoke animatedly. "But I don't want to do that anymore. I want to live my life again the way I did before I got injured, before I saw my friends dying in front of my eyes, because they can't, but I still can, and I don't want to waste the chance I was given."

"Wow, Justin. I...I don't know what to say."

"I started going to a PTSD support group through the VA. It helped me a lot more than those fancy shrinks my mom kept making me see. I'm still going, and I think I'll need to keep going for..."

I cut him off. "It's fine, Justin. You don't have to explain it to me. If it helps you that's all I really care about."

"I'm not all better yet, Jess. I still have nightmares, and I still wake up sometimes and stare at what's left of my legs and I hate them, but I don't want to be away from you for another second. I don't want to wait until I've got myself all sorted out. I know that's selfish, but I love you, Jess. I just want to go back to us."

"Justin, you're not selfish." I felt like I could hardly breathe. "And I don't expect you to be perfect, because I'm not either. All I wanted from you was a chance for us to help each other."

"So that means you won't tell me no all the time when there's something I want to do for you?" I narrowed my eyes at Justin, which he noticed right away. It brought a smile to his face. "What? Are you saying I'm wrong?" he asked.

"No, you're not wrong," I conceded. I hadn't thought about the fact that I'd also refused to let him in entirely. Maybe that was why he hadn't been able to fully trust me. I'd never seen it that way before. "Oh, Justin. I'm sorry, too. It wasn't all your fault that we fell apart."

"You don't need to be sorry. That's the past, and I'm sure we can make things work, Jess, if you give us a chance."

"What happens if we hit some bumps in the road?"

"Then I'll hold on to you real tight."

"Like this?" I scooted closer to Justin and wrapped my arms around him. He felt so warm, I leaned into him and rested my head under his chin inhaling his scent. I felt Justin's chest rise and fall with each breath he took.

"Oh, Jess," he finally said. "I've never wanted anything more than I want you right now."

"Show me."

Justin's lips found mine, and I slowly lowered myself back on the couch with him on top of me. His hands cupped the sides of my face, then he reached for my hair and wrapped his hands in it as he kissed my neck. I slid my hands under Justin's shirt, his back was slick with sweat making his skin feel softer than I remembered, but that was a few months ago, and since then I'd convinced myself that I'd never have him in my arms again. Now that he was, I wanted him more than it felt possible to want someone.

"Justin," I murmured his name.

"What is it, Jess?"

"Is this really happening?"

"It's happening," he whispered and then kissed me again. My breaths came in quick gasps as his tongue teased me. I pulled off Justin's shirt and ran my hands up his sculpted chest. Button by button Justin helped me out of my dress. I lay there staring up at him wearing nothing except my bra and underwear.

"God, you're beautiful," he said.

I reached around my back to unhook my bra and when it was off Justin leaned over me and teased my nipples gently with his tongue. I moaned and reached for him.

"You sure you want to do this now, Jess?'

"Very sure," I breathed.

"Not here. Let's go to the bedroom."

Justin pulled me up and led the way. The rest of our clothes wound up in a heap next to his bed. He lay down first and I got on top of him and guided his hardness inside me. His hands held onto my hips as he swayed beneath me. I shuddered at the feel of him wondering how I'd made it so many months without him. It felt like there was no me and no Justin, like the two of us were one.

As Justin and I lay beside each other afterwards he played with the necklace he'd given me almost a year ago.

"You're still wearing it."

"I could never bring myself to take it off."

It was only our grumbling stomachs that lured us out of bed later that afternoon. We ate lunch together, talked, made love again and then ordered pizza for dinner. It was dark outside by the time I left Justin's apartment. He walked me downstairs and while we waited for a taxi he made me promise I'd be back the next day so we could have dinner together.

Night and day seemed to slow to a crawl as I counted the hours until Justin and I would see each other again. Finally, at four-thirty I got on the train headed towards Manhattan. Justin was already downstairs waiting for me. "What are you hungry for?" he asked after I kissed him.

"Hmmm. I don't know." I wasn't actually hungry at all, but supposed it was probably better that I at least try and eat dinner. "Maybe Chinese?"

"There's a nice restaurant just around the corner from here," he said. "It's pretty casual though."

"You know I don't mind casual."

It took only a few minutes to get to the restaurant. We ordered our food and sat across from each other holding hands across the table. "I missed you, Jess," Justin said.

"I missed you, too."

"I'm not talking about the past couple of months, although I missed you like crazy then too, I'm talking about today. You're the only thing I could think about all day."

"And you think it was any different for me?"

"Then what are we doing here? I just want to be alone with you."

Justin's words were barely out when the waiter came with our food. I smiled at Justin and looked up at our waiter. "You know what, we're going to take that to go."

Ten minutes later we were in the elevator in Justin's building. He pinned me with his body against the back of the elevator while he kissed me. The two of us almost missed getting out on the right floor. Justin unlocked the door to his apartment and I put our take-out cartons in the kitchen as we stepped inside. "I'm not really hungry," I said to Justin. "At least not for food."

He answered me with a kiss. We moved into his bedroom. I lay down and Justin kissed me again. I reached for him, but he held my arms down by my side with his hands. "No," he whispered in my ear. "I want to taste every inch of you first." My body tingled in response to his words. Slowly, he peeled off my clothes and kissed my neck and chest and breasts. He traced his tongue down to my waist and reached between my legs with his hand. I felt like I was on fire. He grabbed my hand with his as he lowered himself to finish his promise to taste every inch of me. I cried out as he made me climax and then again when he entered me. His movements were slow at first, then became more ardent until the both of us climaxed together.

Justin slid beside and kissed the top of my head. He whispered "I love you," but didn't say anything else after that. The feeling of being next to him again was both new and familiar at the same time. My heart, which for the past three months had felt almost as if it weren't a part of me, was whole again. I was so deep in my thoughts that it was only after a while that I realized how quiet Justin had also been. I turned to look at him to see if I could read his thoughts on his face. His eyes were closed, and for a moment I wondered if he'd fallen asleep.

"Justin." I nudged him.

"Hmmm."

"I thought you were sleeping."

"No, I'm not asleep, but I'm afraid to open my eyes because I'm worried that when I do this will have all been a dream, and you'll be gone again."

"I won't be gone."

"You promise?"

"Of course I do."

Justin's eyelids flicked open. "Then it's settled. You'll move in."

"Wait." I sat up slowly as the words Justin just said settled into my mind. "What did you just say?"

"You promised you'd never be gone again."

"You want me to move in with you?" I asked, not believing that's what he'd really said.

"Is it too soon to ask?" Justin looked worried about how I'd answer. I stared at him, taking in his warm brown eyes, soft full lips, the sprinkling of freckles across his cheeks, and I couldn't imagine going another day without seeing him, but I was too stunned to answer him. "Well? Are you going to make me beg, because I will if that's what it's going to take?"

I thought about how hard it had been to leave his apartment the day before, and how long it had felt until we got to see each other again before dinner. It was less than a day, but it had felt like forever. "You don't need to beg." I shook my head, refusing to give myself the chance to overthink things too much. It was crazy, we'd only just gotten back together and there was so much for us still to talk about, but I didn't care. We would have plenty of time for that later. "It's not too soon."

Epilogue

One Year Later

My last year of school seemed to fly by, and graduation day was turning out to be everything I hoped for and more. As I sat and listened to the valedictorian's speech I thought back on the last graduation I'd attended—high school. I'd taken the bus to the ceremony alone. I was probably the only person in my class who didn't have a single friend or family member come to watch them graduate. There was no one to celebrate that day with, but this time around Mike came with Mel, and Justin came with his mother who'd actually taken the day off of work to attend.

Justin wanted to throw me a party at our apartment, but he said his mother insisted on hosting it instead and I agreed. Mrs. Lambert—Allison—she insisted I start to call her, had come around after Justin and I got back together. Justin hadn't been on speaking terms with her, not since our break-up, but I convinced him to forgive her, and she was grateful to me for it. Grateful enough that she apologized for believing the worst about me. She'd told me that she owed me for bringing her son back to her.

After Mike and I gave up our apartment, he moved in with Mel. Their wedding was only a few weeks away. They'd decided on a destination wedding in the Dominican Republic. It would the first real trip away from New York for me and Justin, and I wasn't sure what I was more excited about, being in the Caribbean, or watching my brother get married. Between that, my life with Justin, and the handful of interviews that I'd lined up, it felt like there was so much to look forward to.

Living with Justin had turned out to be even better than I imagined it would be. Justin still surprised me with gifts and fancy dinners, and when my instinct to tell him no came, I reminded myself that it was okay to let him do things for me. At night before we fell asleep the two of us lay beside each other and talked. We talked about his nightmares and the long months it took for him to recover in the hospital after he lost his legs. He'd even brought out his photo albums and I was finally able to see what he'd looked like in his Navy uniform. We also talked about my life, and what it was like to be raised by my crazy father. I told him what living in a group home for four years had been like. I took Justin to his doctors' appointments, and he let me help him when he needed it, and even sometimes when he didn't. Our hearts became irrevocably intertwined as we bared our souls to each other.

It was a perfect June day, so Justin's mother held my celebration outside. It was my first time on a New York rooftop deck. She walked up to me with two glasses of champagne in her hands and handed one to me. "Congratulations, Jessica."

"Thank you."

"To you." She raised her glass and I clinked mine against hers before taking a sip. "I was thinking the other day about how stupid I've been."

"What are you talking about?"

"After I gave birth to Jeff, I wanted a daughter so badly. When the doctor told me James was going to be a boy I cried for months." I still wasn't used to this version of Justin's mother and tried to relax as she spoke. "The other day I was looking through some photos, photos with you in them, and I realized that you've become the daughter I prayed for." She shook her head. "Leave it to Justin to bring you to our family, he always had a way of making me see things differently than I was used to. Our lives feel more complete with you. I'm sorry it took so long for me to see the real you."

"It's okay," I said, touched by her confession.

Justin's eyes caught the two of us talking and he walked over. He was still very protective of me when his mother was around.

"Everything okay?" he asked. He circled his arm around my waist and kissed me on the temple.

"Yes." I turned my head to look at him and smiled. "Everything's perfect."

The End

If you enjoyed Justin and Jessica's story, then you'll want to read Out of Nowhere next to find out what happens to Jessica's best friend Susan and Justin's brother Jeff.

Want to be notified when Teresa Roman's next book will be released? Then sign up for her mailing list by going to http://eepurl.com/ddSrh9. Your email address will never be shared and you can unsubscribe at any time.

Word of mouth and reviews are essential for an author's success. If you enjoyed this book, please consider leaving a review. Even a short review would be helpful and greatly appreciated.

Thank you.

About the Author

Teresa Roman writes contemporary and paranormal romance for adults and young adults. If it was possible to be born with a book in her hands, that's how Teresa would've entered this world. Her passion for reading is what inspired her to become a writer. She loves the way stories can take you to another time and place.

Teresa was born in Romania. She has lived on both coasts of the United States and the Midwest, but currently calls beautiful Sacramento, CA home. She lives there with her husband, three adorable children, two cats and a dog. When she's not at her day job or running around with her kids, you can find her in front of the computer writing, or with her head buried in another book.

Connect with me online.
Website: www.teresaromanwrites.com
Facebook: www.facebook.com/teresaromanauthor
Twitter: www.twitter.com/TRomanauthor
Goodreads: goodreads.com/author/show/14163515.Teresa_Roman
Instagram: www.instagram.com/teresaromanauthor/
Amazon: www.amazon.com/Teresa-Roman/e/B011K661DC/

Acknowledgements

Sometimes I think deciding to write a book was one of the craziest ideas I've ever had, but once the decision was made, there was no turning back. I love books, both reading them, and it turns out, writing them as well. There is just something indescribably magical about books. The road to publication was not an easy one, and I would like to thank everyone that helped me along the way.

Thank you to my husband, Ben, for your support and for being an amazing cheerleader. Thank you to my children who put up with months and months of hearing me say "I swear, I'm almost done with this chapter". Writing has definitely consumed a lot of mommy time, but hearing my kids brag about their mom being an author is always super cute. A special thanks goes to my sister, Elisabeth, who is also my best friend. Don't ever think that I'm not eternally grateful for your beta reading, edits, and words of encouragement.

I would also like to thank Damonza for creating my beautiful book cover and for putting up with my pickiness. It really is appreciated. Thank you to the Kindle Press team, and to everyone who nominated my book and helped my dream of becoming a published author come true. Thank you also to Lisa Reid, for beta reading and cheering me on, and to Brenda Pandos for your writing and publishing advice.

www.ingramcontent.com/pod-product-compliance
Lightning Source LLC
Chambersburg PA
CBHW021005120726
47905CB00009B/2864